WRITERS' BLOC
& BOHOUSE

HOME
TOMORROW
AN ANTHOLOGY OF SHORT STORIES

EDITED BY
JULIAN LAURENCE

6e

www.6epublishing.net

First published in paperback in 2011
by Sixth Element Publishing
Arthur Robinson House
13-14 The Green
Billingham TS23 1EU
Tel: 01642 360253

ISBN 978-1-908299-12-3

British Library Cataloguing in Publication Data. A catalogue record for this book
is available from the British Library.

Printed in Great Britain.

www.6epublishing.net

FOREWORD

Middlesbrough-based landlord and developer Erimus Housing launched its Home Tomorrow writing competition in 2011 to encourage new talent across the Tees Valley and beyond.

Backed by its Bohouse scheme of live/work units for graduates from the creative and digital industries, Erimus, in conjunction with Writers' Block NE, received a record 119 entries.

This compilation is the result of that hard work, showcasing the creative talent of those writers.

Chris Smith, Managing Director of Erimus Housing, said: "We know there's a lot of undiscovered talent out there and we want to help nurture it and bring it to fruition.

"Our Bohouse scheme is all about people making their creativity work for them. Bohouse and its networks of support and knowledge can help their talent work as a business, boosting the local economy and its reputation at the same time.

"We are thrilled with the amount and quality of entries into the competition; the Home Tomorrow theme really captured people's imaginations."

Erimus Housing is a registered housing provider and developer that owns more than 10,500 homes across Middlesbrough, as well as a number in Stockton-on-Tees.

A multiple award winner, Erimus Housing is part of Fabrick Housing Group, along with its partner, Middlesbrough-based Tees Valley Housing.

To find out more about Bohouse log on to www.bohouse.eu or for more information on Erimus Housing, go to www.erimushousing.co.uk

ACKNOWLEDGEMENTS

Many thanks to the Home Tomorrow 500-word short story competition judges: Jo 'Chickamoo' Fairfield (a Bohouse resident and freelance artist from Middlesbrough), Natalie Boxall (BBC Tees), Helen Sturdy (Communications and Media Officer, Fabrick Housing) and Darren Thwaites (Editor, Evening Gazette).

Thank you to Fabrick Housing as a whole, and especially Helen Sturdy who was terrific, inspiring and committed throughout the process!

And thank you to Jacqui Allen who kindly volunteered her time and expertise to proofread the final book.

CONTENTS

TANGERINE GLOW
by Helen Anderson

The last day is the shortest day, whichever way you play it. A sickening understanding stretches out between us. It is over. We know what is ahead of us. It has been closing in from the margins of our consciousness since the very beginning and now there is no place to hide.

It must be faced, head-on. We thought we had forever, but someone pressed fast-forward, and here we are, out of time. It's no use crying about unticked items on my to-do list – all the tastes and sights and experiences I planned to sample. Courage is called for, for all our sakes. There's a lot to be said for a stiff upper lip at times like these.

"Queso!"

Cameras sometimes tell tiny little fibs and so do I. My insides do not mirror my smile. He checks the screen and nods; it is a good one. I can breathe again. He promises that this one will not languish in digital limbo. He swears it will make it to print – maybe a mug or canvas. It will bear witness to the perfection of our existence at precisely 16:42 today. The acrylic blue backdrop is flawless. The light is jaunty and our clothes are deafeningly bright. Strictly no black. We have made a memory that will not fade.

I raise my face up to the paling sun, sucking it in like a monster solar cell, storing up the warmth in my platelets and marrow. I am past caring about wrinkles – too late for me. I stretch out on the cool white bed, listening to the loop of waves crashing over unreal birdsong. I urge myself to let go – to stay – but my mind has already slipped away to the other place.

As I bump to earth, the tangerine glow is unmistakeable. Stepping out into the foggy night, I brace myself. We are back. In the freezing thick of it. My feet shrink in my sandals and my coral pedicure is tinged with guilt. They will be waiting, washed and polished, in snuggly pyjamas. They will be waiting, buzzing with news of their independence and stories of Grandma's funny ways.

They will be waiting to hear how much I have missed them, politely eyeing our luggage.

I feel in my handbag for the key rings and pencils and silk flowers for their hair. We will eat paella for tea in the conservatory, sipping San Miguel, and maybe grey will be okay.

NOT HOME
by Kate Baggott

When I was on maternity leave the second time, my son hadn't started school and my husband travelled for work a lot. One day while he was gone, I was out with the baby and a grandmother in the street scolded me for not having her dressed warmly enough.

"Cover her head," the oma told me. "She'll get pneumonia and end up in the clinic."

It was a beautiful spring morning and everyone was out drinking the sunshine.

"Canadians throw off their seal skins on the first of April," I told her. "We're not weak about weather."

I was offended by her interference. It was typically German and I'd had enough. So, I went home, packed some things and picked up my son from Kindergarten early.

"Let's go see the ocean," I told him.

"Where's the ocean?" he asked.

"Holland!"

The Dutch are the Canadians of Europe. Like us, they let people be themselves. My son didn't know that was important. He also had no idea it would take five hours on two busy highways to reach Holland. He didn't know I'd ask a farmer if I could pitch our tent in a sheltered corner of her pony paddock.

I zipped two sleeping bags together and curled up with my children.

"Isn't this fun?" I asked.

"I missed snack because you picked me up early," my son said.

He whimpered and, because he was distressed, his sister started crying too.

I put my daughter to my breast and spoke gently to both children.

3

"Tomorrow we'll meet the pony and go to the beach," I whispered.

"You better wash the pony shit off my shoe," my son demanded.

"That too," I promised.

Adventure is difficult when you have responsibilities.

"We didn't brush our teeth," my son complained as he fell asleep.

The next morning I cleaned his shoe in dew. The farmer brought us mugs of coffee and hot chocolate.

"You're very kind," I told her.

"You have courage," she told me. "You're leaving your husband?"

"I just need a break from Germany," I explained.

"I understand," she said.

The farmer introduced my children to her pony while I struck camp. I gave her a bottle of maple syrup from the supply I keep in the trunk for helpful souls.

"The coast is windy," she said. "Have you hats for the kids?"

I assured her I had some, somewhere, and she kissed our cheeks three times in farewell.

At the coast, I parked by a spinning windmill and we stopped into a toy shop to buy a red and yellow kite. Finally, we climbed the stairs over the dyke up to the beach.

"Can you see Canada?" my son asked as we looked out over the ocean.

"Wrong direction."

"I almost see it," he shrugged.

"Water," the baby said, her first word.

A man walking his dog helped us get the kite up. We watched it in the wind, freedom on a string, until it was time to go home.

THE DOOR
by Joe Berry

Night fell on the city. A thin blue tear rolled down her cheek as she stood atop the creaking staircase; her emotions had pre-empted the answer to her question, to which several moments of silence had passed. The true love of her story remained fixated not five steps below, feet made of lead. A catch in his throat, stealing the words he longed to find, his body beginning to turn and, with his last ounce of chivalry, closed the door behind him. Anna's eyes fell closed as the latch clicked on the cold oak door. The smooth grey stone steps echoed as Michael made his exit, a sudden moment of hesitation sent the frozen air of the night spiralling around his head, creating a temporary halo which vanished as quickly as it formed, there he stood. Underneath the sanctifying glow of a nearby lamp, Anna sat, her jet black hair edging over the corners of her emerald eyes, her head resting in solitary comfort, against the fresh white railings.

Michael passes through the towering gates out into the street, the glow of the moonlight, covering his shoulders as he grips the railings with a silent hope that he would freeze in this place until the truth came. Suddenly, the street light bursts, the orange sparks of electricity rain down upon him, the hot embers bouncing off the ground, creating an inescapable prison, Michael dares to gaze up until darkness consumes the moment.

Michael, lying on the slated ground, awakens, unable to recognise the very hands that push him up onto his feet. The neon lights of the city guide him away like a siren, as his eyes scan the world like a man lost at an airport terminal.

A moment within his amnesia-ridden mind leads Michael towards the front of an old abandoned dance hall, the rotting timber speaks of its age as Michael leans underneath the barricades to gain entry. The man's eyes witness a monolithic hall, its torn curtains swaying in the breeze, the scuffed floor desolate, aching with its memories. In that moment, ghosts of his past take to the floor, fine gowns and tuxedos spiral, the shredded curtains transform into velvet masterpieces, the dust clears as the floor shines a rich mahogany, a night locked within, comes to life. Amidst the circling couples stands a figure in a ruby red dress, her eyes glancing down as a champagne glass hangs by her side. A chilling sensation fills the air as a mirror reflection of Michael walks through him; the memory takes the hand of the unknown fatal as they dance. Minutes fade to hours, as others disperse, they continue to dance, her smooth ebony hair resting against his shoulder, as the sound of old vinyl scrapes. Morning breaks through the boarded windows and the moment fades away into the yellow morn. Michael takes to the street, his memory restored, running towards the oak door, with the answer to the question which brought about all the grace of a mime… do you love me?

CHRISTMAS FROM LONDON
by Gillian Best

The Mom has few rules in her house, but the most important one, and the one I nearly broke, is that you must turn up for Christmas. There are no excuses. She will fly you from wherever you are, in whatever state of affairs you may be in, to Toronto, and then arrange for a taxi to ferry you back to hers. She doesn't care if your partner's parents want to see you because you'll be at her house. This is not up for discussion.

Foolishly, I suggested recently that since I was going back to the UK in mid-September, and had been living with her for the past six months, that perhaps I might come home in February, or in the spring possibly. I'd barely got the words out of my mouth before she gave me The Death Stare. I had to promise on my life that Christmas morning I would be in her house.

Christmas at The Mom's is a comedy of errors. At some point she decided a good tradition would be to buy a real tree and decorate it at The Sister's house. Which is a fine idea except no one wanted to do it but her. We make every effort to find the worst, saddest looking tree on a nearly barren lot, drag it to The Sister's and then stand around looking at it, as though we were able to will it into an upright position. It falls down several times before The Mom insists we lash it to something sturdy with duct tape and twine.

Then we move on to Christmas morning, whereupon her three cranky and poorly-rested children, suffering from various stages of jetlag and hangovers, shuffle downstairs to have an argument over coffee and breakfast. The Brother makes a breakfast that would stop your heart; The Sister complains about the smell of bacon cooking. I try to be pleasant and that involves a lot of not saying anything.

We then retire to the formal living room and begin opening gifts. Which is always very exciting. For The Mom the best part is taking terrible photos with a disposable camera.

Here's the irony in that one, Dear Reader: each of her children has a very good digital camera. The environmentally-conscious Mom throws caution and David Suzuki to the wind while snapping away with abandon. These pictures, which are the only ones she takes all year, are mostly of the pets.

Yes, for us, Christmas is a series of bad jokes. The worse the joke, the more we like it.

And for this, I fly from London, through Amsterdam to Montreal and then Toronto. But coming home at Christmas is the only way you can keep The Mom from cancelling your passport.

HOME TOMORROW
by Patrick Brereton

Donna paced the kitchen, blowing deeply drawn clouds of nicotine-infused smoke into the small space she had occupied for the past two hours.

Home tomorrow. The thought assaulted her as she paced the kitchen.

"She's been in there forever," said Donna's son, Tommy, as he peered through the fog of cigarette smoke enveloping his mother.

"She's scared, Tommy."

He turned to his younger sister who was sharing the anxiety of her mother. He didn't say anything; he simply crossed and held her close.

Donna watched as her kids offered each other the support that she was meant to give. It was perhaps at that moment that she turned from self-pity mode into caring mother mode.

"You bastard. You're not doing this to my kids, not again!"

"Don't suppose you'll be out for long, Nosher?" offered one prison officer.

Nosher ignored the attempt to goad him into a physical reaction that had seen his prison sentence increased three times in the past two years.

"Might pop round to see your lass next time you're on nights, screw."

The prison officer smirked as other prisoners cheered Nosher on. Anybody who got one over on the screws was always going to be a cause célèbre. That and the fact that Nosher was the hardest man in the place and even on his last day inside, it was a good idea to keep on his good side.

"Good job ya didn't smack 'im one Nosh, they'd 'ave had you banged up for another three weeks for it." The younger prisoner was half jogging behind and to each side of his hero as he made his way back to his cell. Nosher quickly began to tire of him.

He stopped suddenly and spun round, causing the younger man to collide with him. Nosher eyeballed him as he quickly backed away.

"My eldest will be about your age, well, from what I remember."

"Yea, younger, more agile, I wonder? Go on, take a swing."

"You what Nosh?"

"I'll give you a free shot, just the one, unless you are very, very quick." Nosher stood perfectly still.

The younger man took a pace back. "Give over Nosher, I'm not that daft, nor is anyone else here."

Nosher smiled.

Donna finally left the sanctum of the kitchen, approached her kids and unashamedly burst into floods of tears.

"Don't worry, Mam," said Zoe.

"Yeah, we were just kids last time, Mam, "added Tommy. "We won't stand around and let him hurt you again. This is our home, not his."

Donna fell into their arms.

"Welcome home," thought Nosher as he stood outside his front door. He didn't knock. He didn't announce his presence; he simply leant back and with one vicious kick, knocked the door off its hinges.

Donna sat on the sofa as a shiver ranged itself up and down her spine.

Nosher strode confidently and arrogantly into the front room, an empty front room.

"Don't worry, Mam," said Zoe. "He'll never find us here."

HOME?
by Kathryn Brown

Eileen left for the dentist that morning thinking the only thing she had to worry about was a filling. Sometimes life becomes surreal. There's nothing you can do about it, you just have to accept this and hope that when the dust settles, you remain standing. Speaking of dust, there was quite a lot of it about when Eileen returned. She did a double take, I mean you can forget where you leave your car from time to time but not your house. Think about it. If a postman goes to a certain street looking for No.126, he expects to find it in the same place today as yesterday. He doesn't expect to have to go looking for it.

Anyway, Eileen returns complete with filling one hour later and there is no sign of her house. There is a lot of dust and debris and she'll admit herself she can be careless and a bit through-other at times but this is just ridiculous.

She doesn't need to ring the emergency services, they are already there.

The good news is she didn't have a husband in the property when it decided to fold in on itself, nor a dog or cat come to that, so at least there were no fatalities.

She rings Sue on her mobile. Sue will know what to do.

"Hello. Sue, it's Eileen. I've got a bit of a problem."

"What is it, Eileen? Your voice sounds a little strange. Are you okay?"

"Pretty good considering. I appear to have lost my house."

"What do you mean? Eileen, where are you? I'll come and pick you up. Just tell me where you are?"

"I'm standing in my front garden at present."

"What do you mean? You're at home? Why aren't you inside? Have you forgotten your key? It's raining."

"True, though it's only a slight drizzle."

"Eileen. I'm coming over. I'll be with you in ten minutes."

Surveying the wreckage and answering their questions as best she could, Eileen thought of all the years she had spent alone in that house and suddenly felt a huge sense of relief. She realised that she was looking forward to a change. None of the messy business of selling was required. She could have a change without having to decide anything at all. She smiled.

Sue arrived, jumped from the car and rushed over to Eileen.

"My God Eileen, my God. What… what the hell happened?"

"I've absolutely no idea," murmured her friend. "When I left home this morning, I closed my front door as usual. When I returned," she indicated with a gesture, "this is what I found. I've simply no idea how it happened. Isn't it funny? Could you ever have imagined such a thing?"

Sue judged her friend to be in shock. "Eileen. I'm taking you home. I'll leave these gentlemen my number and they can get in touch with you there."

As they drove away, Eileen noticed that her tooth was hurting.

LATE NIGHT POKER
by Jonny Bussell

He's got nothing. He's definitely got nothing, Simon kept telling himself. The other side of his brain was also telling him, I've got nothing, absolutely nothing. Gav was messing with two chips in his left hand, that's his tell. He definitely had nothing but Simon only had a pair of fours. Was he going to put his last £50 in?

•

Why Simon moved to London on reflection is now unclear. There was nonsense spoken of living the dream and going for it. In the end he was just a daft bloke from Boro working in a bar where all his colleagues were Polish. He missed everything about home. He missed Kerry, he missed his Mam and he missed the rain. As the Guinness glass filled he tried to make a shamrock but it looked more like a cock and balls. Typical. Four hours to go till poker. Three hours fifty nine minutes till poker.

•

It started as a bit of fun between four lads from the North East on a Saturday night but it quickly got serious. From betting using chips and everyone putting in a fiver for the first few weeks, the hands were now unlimited and the lads were getting more and more competitive as each week went by. Gav had taken Ben's wedding ring last week with three Jacks and Ste had taken Shaun's iPod the week before with a Flush. In went Simon's last fifty quid. As he put it in he realised he'd have to work the best part of nine hours for that fifty quid. Simon hoped and hoped Gav had nothing.

•

It was quite generous of Simon's boss Carl, a thick Aussie with stupid hair, to let the lads play poker every Saturday night in the pub. It was very generous of him to be incompetent which allowed the boys to have as much booze as they could neck without him being any the wiser.

•

Gav raised Simon by another fifty quid. Simon had nothing but couldn't back out now. He couldn't just wave goodbye to two hundred and twenty quid like that. He chucked in his train ticket home to Boro, fifty pounds including Young Person Railcard discount. Gav slowly turned over his cards.

•

Gav had a tear in his eye as he pulled in to Middlesbrough train station, his Mam waiting to greet him. He loved being home for the weekend. He caught up with friends and family. It would be the last time he'd see his Gran before she passed away a month later although he didn't know it at the time. Gav remembered how much he loved his hometown and how that love will never change no matter how long he stays away. He had a tear in his eye.

•

Simon filled pint after pint. Forty five hours it would take to make that back. A pair of fives. He knew Gav had nothing.

HOME TOMORROW
by Carol Butler

"Come on Joe, one last time." Isla's eyes flashed with encouragement.

Joe looked up. "I've heard that one before!" he said, giving a wry smile.

"I mean it this time; you're doing so well today. One more try then I'll take you back to the ward."

Joe raised himself up from his chair and grabbed onto the bars. Slowly he put one foot in front of the other and shuffled along until he reached the end.

"Whoo hoo!" Isla yelled. "That was your best yet – we'll have you letting go soon!"

Joe wasn't quite so confident – he still had little feeling in his legs. Now and again he felt his toes tingling and the doctors were very encouraging, assuring him this was a positive sign.

They were careful though, Joe knew, not to give any false hope, never going as far as to say he would be able to walk again on his own.

Isla took Joe back to the ward and helped him settle into his bed.

"See you tomorrow, champ," she said as she waved goodbye. "Not long before visiting time. Be sure to tell Amy how well you did today."

Amy. Joe thought about his wife. She had been fantastic, visiting every day through all the months, always with a beaming smile on her face. But Joe knew that, for most of the time anyway, the smile was false.

They still hadn't really talked about him coming home. Hadn't faced the realities of him in a wheelchair. Maybe for the rest of his life. What about all their plans? They would have to talk about it soon – the doctors were coming later to tell him when he was likely to be discharged. Still quite a while yet though, he guessed.

Amy sat at the kitchen table, her coffee going cold. It would soon be time for her to go to the hospital. She thought back to last night.

"Amy, honey, I'm sorry to keep on, but when are you going to tell him?" David asked for the umpteenth time.

"I'm trying," Amy shot back, "but it's difficult. He is so down. I know his cheery greeting and his chat is mostly an act. He so looks forward to my visits – it's all he has."

"I know how hard it is," David insisted, "but you owe it to yourself and to me to tell him. If he's expecting to come back home and be with you, it's better to tell him whilst he still has time to adjust."

Amy had ended up promising David she would tell him today. Quite how, she didn't know.

It had all been so unexpected and sudden with David. But she had no doubts, just guilt when she thought of Joe and all the dreams they had had for their future.

Amy fixed her smile and walked into the ward. She saw Joe look up and beam.

"Fantastic news Amy – the doctors say I can come home tomorrow."

HOME TOMORROW
by David Butler

I t was June 1991 – it was hot and sticky, in a downtown Manama call box, Bahrain.

"I'll be home tomorrow," I said… finally reunited with my family whom I had only seen for five days in nine months, during the 1st Gulf War.

Working around the clock from September 1990 – we made 'invisible' Tornados (don't ask how, as I would have to shoot you!) for urgent dispatch to the Middle East front line. Like many other happy chappies, (not!) I found myself in deepest, darkest Suffolk, at RAF Honington.

Many other colleagues had been in theatre on Op Granby/Desert Storm/Desert Shield since August, yet I myself, only 70 miles away from my wife and daughter, may just as well have been catching some sun in the Gulf, albeit under some pressure.

Slogging 16 hour shifts, and freezing our little wotsits off wasn't exactly my idea of heaven.

Christmas came and went – with me, (one of the lucky ones) getting five days back at my base, full of cold, and just in time to pack my bags, for a posting to snowbound Germany.

Midway through February, we were preparing to deploy to Muharraq in Bahrain, whilst colleagues were right in the thick of Scud Missiles. Meanwhile, my family had to pack up and move themselves, lock stock and no smoking barrels, to a married quarter in North Rheine Westphalia.

On arrival in Manama, the accommodation was deceptively salubrious, compared to many – although it wasn't very long before the stench of a defunct air-conditioning system made it a joy to go to work on base, where we had air-conditioned cabins inside the hangar.

March came and went (and my wife and daughter's birthdays) –

then the official ceasefire was signed in April – but old Saddam was still being naughty to the Kurds up in the North, so we needed to keep a patrol presence in the air.

Toward the end of April, however, we were packing up – giving us every indication we just might be home soon. Then the pantomime season really kicked in!

As some army units were still pitching up out of the desert, and the oily rain continued to fall – it was understandable, when we got to the airport lounge (with full kit) – only to be told to "Foxtrot Oscar" (a polite beloved Forces phrase, for being told to fuck off).

However, when we were turned away for a second time – it did seem as if somebody up there really didn't like us. Of course, on both occasions, many of us had rang home – getting everyone excited at the other end – only to be desperately disappointed.

May '91 came and went and, for the third time of asking, we were bussed up to the airport lounge, only to be rejected (yet again)! Now some of our patience was beginning to wane – when all of a sudden, an Army (yes Army) Lieutenant Colonel, appeared – and insisted he was getting on the plane – and bless him – he was taking us lot with him!

Everybody got on the phones, saying, "we will be home tomorrow!"

This is dedicated to all our servicemen and their families – especially those who do not return home.

18

HOME TOMORROW
by Keith Butler

Today is a good day, filled with memories. Not the big fish and chip, Punch and Judy, seaside sandcastle memories but the little ones.

I'm sitting on the patio: a tartan rug across my knees and looking at the daisy dappled, buttercup beautiful meadow, swaying in the sun speckled soft sigh of a salt breeze.

An autumn evening: nursing thoughts of fireworks and Christmas, the smell of family fires' smoke in the air, watching starlings start their kaleidoscope swoop and storm across the darkening sky.

McIlroy's dancehall: dancing with that beautiful girl, The Tremeloes singing 'Even the Bad times are Good'. I walked her home and missed the last bus. We kissed goodnight. I didn't want that soft kiss to end.

First year of Infant School: daisies are our silver, buttercups our gold and I saw pictures painted with words. The infant rebel wouldn't accept that these were the only treasures that we could hold.

Standing in a playground corner, spring sun on my face, warm rough red brick at my back, wearing trousers made from Granny's old skirt. Shiny serge sackcloth saw toothing at my tender legs. I peed them rather than face the fear filled boys' bogs.

I think that I used to work with words, painting pictures for others to see.

When I first came here I used to piss myself to get back at the carers who didn't. But they knew and left me in my soaking, stained pyjamas and I had to find other ways to equal the score. That's when I started my treasure horde; a pencil, some paper clips that I linked together like a daisy chain, a red felt tipped pen, some plasters and a furry polo all carefully stolen from the nurses' station. I hid them in my locker, all the treasure I could have or hold.

It didn't stop Mrs Blazinski though. She still pinched and pummelled us pathetic pyjama-ed patients, who beseeched her to stop with imploring eyes and silent-movie mouths.

I think that my mother came yesterday. Not the weary work-worn mum but the beacon-beaming beautiful wedding photo faced mum. Perhaps the bad days aren't so bad.

I took my revenge today. Under the sign that says 'The Management accept no responsibility for the loss of valuables and clothing' I wrote in furious felt tipped letters, 'What about our pride and self respect?'

I blazoned my slogan in red shaky screaming letters across the wall. I shouldn't have signed it though. They've taken away my treasure now, nothing to have or hold.

They said I was disruptive and they would have to speak to my children.

I wonder if they might send me home tomorrow.

That would be a good day!

THE SISTERS OF HOME HEATH
by Victor Cage

There were the trees. The forest of green, but pale, like it was slowly being chased away. And there was the wind. The wind was haunted, and angry, and often couldn't contain its anguish over what its precious innards had become. And the darkness. The darkness was the worst possible thing in existence. This darkness was yet to come. It was so alike a horizon, just waiting to come forth. Allowing men to go mad before the looming approach. It covered their lives, and their families, and their homes, and the days of old. And yet, despite the rapture of pale, or the spite of the wind, or the cunning of the darkness, they were all set. They all knew who they were, and were aware of their places, and felt at home. In fact, the pale and the wind often clubbed together and spoke ill of the darkness behind his back. But nonetheless, home was their individual virtue.

And with that passing thought, the fog parted, and five horses appeared a distant depth away.

And atop them rode five figures. Five of the most beautiful figures you could ever possibly imagine. Five sisters riding from the chaos that had destroyed their ideas of home. And their faces told stories of utter dread.

Alyssis, Mina, Kyra, Sephie and Rosa as I recall. In fact, I do recall the calling of names aloud. Such soft tones, and with tenderness in their voices. So sad, then, that their stories had led them here, without home and without hope.

And, yes. And Alyssis. A silent thought of Mother's last wishes:

"Please, my Angel, take good care of your Sisters. They are weak in the eyes of the storm, and they must have you to guide them. They will not survive without you."

Her tears bore no ill will; only wishes to go back to an elder time. "If only time were as it was," came the thought not unlike the darts of war. It was a sharp thought, and one that left unstrained memories lingering.

"If one wish were to come true, let it only be for the smallest of berries and fruits from the trees. We've rid ourselves of the last of the bread, and I fear…" spoke Rosa, gently interrupted by Mina, who concurred, "It's been longer that we've been without even half the measure of a drop than I'd care to remember."

"We should have stayed. We should have stayed to fight," argued Kyra, strength in her case as a red sky set.

Mina was growing cold, "I miss home," to which Sephie came to the notion that home was the land which held her sister's feet, and the air which gave life to her sister's heart.

"We'll find ourselves a new home tomorrow," each convinced herself.

Alyssis couldn't help but agree. Silently, of course. For in her own heart she was unsure or even petrified of whether Home actually existed anymore, or even whether tomorrow would come.

HOME TOMORROW
by Michael Cail

You don't mind if I sit here, do you? My flight is delayed and I need a sit down; this case weighs a ton! My Dad's not very well so I'm going home tomorrow to see him. Well, not really home, because home's here. That doesn't really make sense, does it? Let me explain.

After I finished college I did what a lot of kids in England do at that age (listen to me: "kids" – I'm only twenty-three myself) and went to work at Camp America. It was a lot of fun and I got to meet a lot of interesting people. Like Tyler. He liked the same music I did, had read the same books and yeah, okay, he was quite fit and I seemed to be spending more and more time with him.

The night before we were due to leave camp, he asked me what I was doing and I told him I was going on to New York. He told me that he lived in New Jersey and asked if I wanted to stay with him. When I said yes, he gave me this grin that took over his whole face; an adorable cartoon smile.

We had so much fun together and before I left for England, we swapped e-mail addresses and promised to stay in touch, like you do. I didn't expect anything. I figured it would be one of those holiday romance things and when you get home, it starts with an e-mail every day, then every other day, then every week and, well, you get the idea. You've probably done it yourself.

What I didn't expect was to be back two months later, spending the Thanksgiving holiday in the shadow of the skyscrapers of Manhattan. Tyler and I picked up from where we left off, and went a little bit further too. I begged, stole and borrowed to get back (not literally!) and when I got there, it was becoming harder and harder to leave because my idea of "home" was beginning to change, shifting away from England. I felt more at home in America and more alive with Tyler.

No matter how excited I was that Tyler felt the same way, I dreaded telling my parents that I was going to emigrate, especially my Mum. I could guess her reaction because we're cut from the same cloth; she didn't disappoint. Dad served as umpire during the slanging matches, torn between his first love and his first-born. He was always much cooler than Mum, and told me I should do what made me happy; I'd never loved him more. That's why I'm going back, because I'm not sure how poorly he is. Mum was really vague but she's been like that since I left, so I'm not sure what to make of it.

Anyway my plane is at the gate, so I'll have to get going. I've told Mum I'll be home tomorrow. I don't think I meant it.

I'LL BE HOME TOMORROW
by AJ Campbell

She was a mere girl when she first met him. He had charmed her, wined and dined her. He was dazzling, incredible, a lot older, he knew the world, a real man, her first love. They married soon after, this was for keeps, nearly thirty years ago.

She was used to him being strong, always the one in control. As he lay in the hospital bed he looked so weak, so sick and vulnerable.

He seemed delirious, mumbling, in a distant dreamland apparently reliving his life, revisiting places. Some of them were familiar to her, but then he was talking about leaving a farm, the family were at the gate. It seemed like yesterday to him, but it was a lifetime ago. It meant nothing to her, the place or the people; he hadn't reached their life yet!

He was suddenly wide awake, alert, vividly talking to her about people and places, some still mysteries to her, other segments warm and familiar, wonderful, the best parts of their lives together.

As she turned to leave, he affectionately called her name. She was startled, but she didn't know why!

She watched him. He seemed to know. The operation had at first seemed to have gone very well. The doctors said they were pleased, then the infection had quickly taken hold. He was now losing this fight.

She felt numb as she left the hospital. She could hardly drive home and the tears were clouding her eyes. She should really have stopped, pulled in to compose herself.

She couldn't face going straight home to the rest of the family, the kids and now their children, their grandchildren, ages and generations seemed confused. She was confused, couldn't think straight, still thinking of her daughter as a child, not the mother of her grandchildren.

On a whim she changed direction and headed for the park, the same park the whole family had loved ambling through.

At first she couldn't think at all, oblivious to the dog walkers, distracted by the woodpecker hammering away, then she saw the family of swans in the lake. They were beautiful. Her thoughts returned to her family, and husband.

She instinctively knew that he wasn't coming home, that was why he called out her name as she was leaving. He never called out her name. It was always, "pet", or "darling". It seemed so final!

She was now in her fifties, wishing she could go back in time. She had barely finished being a teenager when they met, her life had been him, and he had always looked after her.

She would have to make all the decisions now.

What would she say to the family? Should she tell the truth as she saw it, or go along with his version that he would be "home tomorrow"?

SURFACING
by Jake Campbell

Lloyd went round the world four times and never saw it. Between a surveillance operation in Hudson Bay and active duty in the cosmos of the Atlantic, his travels under the Earth's cling-film of seas were a master class in black-hole weightlessness. How the hum of the engines became the frolicking of cows in Flora-perfect fields; how the silence when they switched them off and waited on the sandy floor of the Pacific made him feel like a witness at the end of the Triassic period, waiting for Pangea to crack. At night, the Polaroid of his daughter grew arms and legs, became a raised puppet that clopped through his dreams, but fell limp to the floor as soon as his lids split.

Arriving at his welcome home party in their local, Lloyd sipped a Schweppes bitter lemon with his high-school friend, Harry.

"Well, you haven't missed much, that's for sure," joked Harry.

Lloyd swilled his glass, rattling the ice-cubes. Harry scratched the back of his head.

"So, your pension must be pretty nifty?"

"Look, Harry, I've just come up…"

Harry stood, placed a hand on Lloyd's shoulder, smiled then went back to the bar.

His nephew ran over. "Do you want a game of Battleships, Uncle Lloyd?"

Lloyd felt his cheeks flush. "I…yes, but you'll have to remi…"

"It's easy," said the nephew. He overturned two beer mats and handed Lloyd a yellow Bic with the end chewed.

Later that night, as he gargled Corsodyl, his wife tried to discuss their life insurance policy and whether he thought the Mégane was past it.

"Whatever," he grumbled, taking off his watch and placing it on the bedside table.

"Lloyd?"

Lloyd remembered the tone. It was the same one she adopted when he'd docked in Manitoba. He'd rung, listened as she talked listlessly about her sister's new baby, before snorting hard, with the kind of phlmp the sun might make as it begins to supernova, then on the exhale, "Lloyd? It's Banister. Phlmp. They had to put him down."

He'd scratched the toonie on the coin slot, half pushed it in, held, withdrew, stuffed it back in his pocket, asked if she was alright; said at least the bugger's out of his misery, then, I have to go, dear, it's going to click out any minute. I lo…

"Lloyd? Are you listening?"

"Hmmph?"

"Are you alright?"

"Fine. Thanks."

He pulled the duvet up and rolled over.

Several hours later, his wife felt the nail-file of Lloyd's sideburn rustling in the gap of her nightie; his ear pressed to the sonar pulse of her thorax.

"Lloyd, darling, what's…" she said, running her palm through his hair.

"Shh. Listen. Can you hear it?"

I KNOW, IT'S JUST THAT
I CAN'T TELL YOU
by Bill Carr

I hope to be home tomorrow but then I've been hoping so every day for the last four weeks.

I was in the garden, tidying up. Dead-heading roses, their bloom faded, like mine. One minute I'm bent over, the next – wham! A massive surging pain in my head. Like a bomb had gone off inside my skull, the shockwaves rippling around my cranium. A big bleed they said, buggering up my brain. A stroke. Where did that soft word come from for something so devastating? My neighbour's girl found me, bless her. Though I wished she hadn't, God forgive me.

So I've lain here in hospital for over four weeks, waiting to go home but unable to say so. I know all, understand all, my senses working all too well. Smell, sight, taste, touch and hearing all turbo boosted. Their functions cruelly sharpened as I can't speak or even move except for one side of my face. So when I try to speak it's like a drunken slur.

There's so much I want to say, simple things like "my nose is itchy, please scratch it" to complicated like "I love you, forgive me" to my girls. My words stay stored inside my poor head, like students kettled at a protest. Except I don't even have a banner to wave and complain. So the words queue up, jostling and bumping against each other while my mind cries out. Occasionally a word will form on my lips when I have a visitor and I try to tell them something but they try to guess to help me, it all goes wrong and I end up swearing. That's not like her, they tell the staff. It must be the stroke. Of course it's the stroke. The stroke is everything.

If only I could go home tomorrow, I'd be okay. Here everything is noisy. Loud television, stupid people shouting at each other. I'm surrounded by strangers. Coughing, bleeding, dying. I'm not getting better and I'm not going to. I just want to go home. To peace and quiet, surrounded by my things. My own chair, own radio, own garden, own bed. The photos of my family, my wedding photo, children, grandchildren.

It depends on the assessment, they say. I want to tell them I don't care about the assessment. I've refused food for two weeks now rather than live like this. Turning my face to the wall they've called it. The nice nurse told my daughters she's seen this before. Stroke victims switching off. I'm trying to say I've had enough. Now let me go home and live out my days peacefully.

If I could speak I'd explain that the right thing for me is to go home. If not today, then let me go home tomorrow. Bring my family around, let them kiss me goodbye. I'd force the words out. Thank you. I'm happy to go now. If I could go home tomorrow it would be just perfect.

BOLDLY COMING HOME
by Dave Clark

"Captain, we're entering the solar system," said Hans, my official deputy, the words almost trembling out of his throat. It was an emotional time.

"Let me see," I said to Wanda, his wife. She flicked a switch and the solar system spread out before us on screen. Barely visible, at the far end, a bright, distant dot, our home. Just a day away.

Our mission had taken 33 years. We'd hoped to solve the greatest mysteries of science. The problems of dark matter, the rate of expansion of the universe, the fate of black holes. By taking measurements from other star systems it was hoped that we'd be able to identify errors in the readings from Earth and produce a definitive unified theory of everything. The data we'd collected would keep Earth's scientists busy for decades.

However, because of the speed we were travelling, from the perspective of the Earth's residents we had been away for over 2,000 years, such are the oddities of space-time. We shared an unspoken fear that, since we've been gone, science would have solved all of these mysteries and our mission would prove pointless.

I opened the radio transmitter. "Hello planet Earth, this is Voyager 1256 returning home."

"Hello everyone," Hans shouted over my shoulder.

"Say hello, Wanda."

"Hello everyone."

I switched off, waiting for a reply.

Visiting new solar systems had been a thrill that made the monotony of the journey there seem almost worthwhile. We had visited Alpha Centauri A and B, then on to Barnard's Star and Ross 154 then back to Earth. I also got the opportunity to be the first person in human history to step foot on a planet outside our own solar system. We landed and took samples of Tiny Centauri. Pity it was such a dump though, a dry, rock ball with no atmosphere.

"Any response yet?" I asked Wanda. She shook her head, we'd had no response to our messages. I said nothing to Wanda and Hans, but feared the worse. The Earth is silent, no response to our messages, not even a beeping satellite or TV signal. Somehow, during our 2,000 year absence, mankind has contrived to destroy itself.

The last ten years, the journey home, have been particularly hard, with no exploration to look forward to. We've grown old and disillusioned together.

Hans and Wanda barely talk to each other now. It had been a fairytale romance, starting shortly after we launched, but it gradually soured. The monotony of space travel can do that to a couple, hell, it could do it to an individual's very soul. They had tried for kids, but it had proved impossible, whether it was them or a peculiarity of space travel, we never established.

On the screen the blue/green planet is clearly visible now. This is the view I remember from my first mission to Mars. This is home.

I send another message, "Voyager 1256 returning", but the responding silence is deafening.

SURF'S UP
by Anne Colledge

"Surf's up," Pete shouted.

Jane dragged her damp wet suit on with disgust. Why did she do this to herself? It was something about feeling the fear but still doing it. It was a new challenge she needed all the time. Her boyfriend worried about her. "Be careful," he said when she left.

"Let's do it," Pete shouted. They could hear the surf pounding onto the shore.

Her kayak went crazy in the waves as they crashed in, but the sea smelled like seaweed and seashells and fish mixed up together. A deep breath made her feel really alive. She had to keep the nose of the boat into the waves or she would capsize. A huge wave washed over her, soaking her and covering the deck of her boat. White salty water full of bubbles.

"Come on, further out. You just need confidence, that's all."

Jane was not sure. She was frightened and paddled like mad to get away from the rocks on her right. If the sea got her sideways she would be in. She turned and looked behind. A big wave was breaking behind her.

Pete shouted, "Stern rudder," but it was too late. She was under the boat then up and grabbed a breath. Then under again. It was like being in a washing machine.

Pete shouted, "Pull the deck off and get out."

She got back in and watched for a wave. Pete came hurtling past her right up to the beach. Wonderful. The next one had her name on it. She screamed with pleasure on the front of the wave and felt the power and the force of it rushing up the beach. It was like the fun fair, on the Big Dipper when she was a child. Wonderful. She shouted, "I did it!"

She sang, "I'm riding along on the crest of a wave."

As they crossed the harbour on the way back, a small fishing boat came chugging back in.

"I expect they think we're worse than mad going out in a boat for pleasure. They'd rather be down the club or watching footie on the telly with a pint of beer in their hand if they could. Not that we don't like that as well."

The black seal poked his head up like a large dog beside them. "The seal likes it here." She could see down his nostrils and he had huge brown eyes.

Her hands were so cold that she had a job to get her wet kit off but the hot shower was heaven. She could have stayed in it forever and when she got out she felt really alive. Like Pete said, "It's not the exercise it's the rest after it."

Her phone rang. It was her boyfriend, "You still alive then? I don't need to bring the body bag."

"You always exaggerate."

"When will you be home?"

"Tomorrow. See you then."

"Ready for the pub?" Pete shouted.

LITTLE SPIDER
by Charly Conquest

I was driving. That's me story. I was just driving.

That's all I ever do. I wouldn't say I was driving home 'cos I'm not so much one of them that has a proper home. I don't like to put down roots I might get tangled in.

I'd picked up a lass 'night before and promised her as far as Bristol. When he pulled me over I thought that were why.

"Officer," I says, "she's me daughter."

But she were gone, scarpered like out a trap. Cop points out me headlamps blinking and I thinks, "well, that's cost me a bit o' company for 50 miles now."

Then I hears it. Tap, tap, tap. Then "shhh". Then nothing.

Comes from the back of me truck. I thinks, "blinking lights don't sound nowt like that."

There they were. Five of 'em. All the colour of tea when you've left the bag in too long. Just staring at me. Reminded me of what me Mam used to say about spiders:

They're more scared of you, Jim, than you are of them.

So I beckons 'em up, flat hand like I do with the old knacker ponies down the yard. It's smallest one what comes. 'Cos he doesn't know he's at the glue factory. He shoves some paper at me. A map. A map. The cheek!

"I'm not a taxi," I says. But the little one don't know. It's just noises to him. Face doesn't twitch. Hand doesn't move. It's up on the Moors he's pointing and I coaxes his little spider-fingers off to see. Church. Church on the Moors.

Five of 'em. Not a job between 'em. Wants me to drive 'em to Church. I read papers, I know what them lot does for their God.

"Get out," I points. I'm not having no more of this not understanding.

Dad Tea Bag steps forward. I don't so much want his argument.

35

"Church," he says. Dead quiet. He looks paler in the light. Not his skin, just in his eyes.

I thinks I must be mad, sad or both. I thinks I'm going to chuck 'em all out. But I sees your man again and I shut the door. Don't want 'em in there, but no reason to see the lit'lens split from all they ever known.

I dunno why I drives 'em there. Fuel 'ent cheap. Maybes I was making up for the bad things. But I done it. Right up on them Moors and no further. That's your lot.

I was ready to slam the door on 'em. Five little darkie scallions.

'Cept it was six. Six little dark ones. One's not moving. And they lays her out on the ground. She were no bigger than a dot. Palest one of all. Carries her in.

They says thank you. Only word little spider knew.

I checked the truck again. No more. It were like a sauna in there…

Anyways, that's when I thought I'd better call you lot back.

WALKING THESE BLUES
by Bud Craig

One foot in front of the other. Steady away, talking to Fats Domino. Courtesy of mp3 technology, Fats, your huskily caressing voice sings in my ears about someone "walking these blues". That's what I'm doing, I suppose. Why did you record a song called 'Walking to New Orleans' when you live there? Mind, I've no room to talk. I'm on the fourth leg of the Lovendale Way – 72 miles in five days – and I've lived in Lovendale all my life. The North East of England's the best place this time of year, plenty of daylight.

In case you're wondering why I'm walking on my own, Fats, my wife, Carol, has got another bloke. As soon as I knew, I had to get away. There was no time to contact anybody else. Anyway, I knew for a fact my mate, Rob, couldn't make it and George, my son, has just started a new job in London. I thought the walking might help, as well as keeping me in shape. Maybe I'll write a book: Fitness for Cuckolds.

The steep sides give the valley an intimate, self-contained feel as though the rest of the world doesn't exist. The Lovendale Hills, millions of years old, roll into the distance, melting into one another like lovers. Kind of puts things into perspective, Fats. Or maybe not.

The good news is I've no money worries – I banked my redundancy cheque on Friday. Sod Valley Engineering, I think to myself, and sod Carol, as the sun gradually nudges aside a bank of pale cloud. The honey smell of cut grass mingles with the fragrance of May blossom. A lark warbles up above, harmonising with the quee-quee of a curlew in the distance. Lovely.

Getting to the top of Swanny Fell was the hardest bit, but it's worth it for the views. Now it's an easy stretch on the level before a stroll down a gentle gradient to the Brown Cow in Alderton.

I expected my life to be like that. It was meant to be downhill all the way from now on. Shows how much I know. I'm thinking of Carol and Rob as I go through the flowering meadows. Did I tell you I caught her and my lifelong pal on the living room floor? At it. I don't know what was the worst part: the otherworldly noises coming out of her mouth, the eczema scar on his arse or the 'Girl of My Best Friend' corniness of it all. Will I ever be able to listen to Elvis again, I wonder.

I'll have a few pints tonight and a full English in the morning. Should set me up for the last leg. What then, Fats? Go home and face the music? Someone must have found the bodies by now. Or maybe I'll do the Lovendale Way again, the other way round this time. Just keep on walking. Walking these blues.

WAITING
by Carolann Creagh

Pulling the key from the front door, Emma walked over the small scattering of mail under foot. Gasping for a cuppa, getting the kettle on was her bigger priority over sifting through the usual bills, circulars and junk mail that fed its way through her shiny bronze letterbox on a daily basis.

It had been busy in work and she'd had no time to draw breath, let alone drink a coffee. So it was only when she had cup out, spoon at the ready and the almost boiled kettle was humming away, did she retrieve the small bundle from the hall mat a few steps away.

But suddenly the boiling water didn't matter and the aromatic dark roast beans lost their appeal. Her eyes caught the brown buff envelope peeking out between her bank statement and a yellow plastic charity bag. Small and insignificant, the hospital name and cancer centre stamp could just be made out in the left hand corner. A familiar name glaring back at her through the tiny window box. She didn't want this name; she wanted it to be a postal error meant for a Jane Brown or a Mary Smith, for anybody but Emma Procter. A lump now formed so large in the back of her throat she thought she might suffocate and drown in her own saliva. Pulse racing, she ripped at the stringy gum, not paying any attention to the paper cut now forming and smarting on her index finger.

Liver scan 9.40! Another scan? Why?

Ten short days earlier she had held her breath in the CAT scan machine as a dye careered its way through her system, mapping her organs. Trying to manage her intense fear of enclosed spaces, she had given little thought or consideration to the results. Her priority was getting out of that tube. One wrong breath would only prolong her terror. So for 20 long minutes she studied the curved tomb-like roof a few inches above her nose. Emma couldn't decide whether to be amused or annoyed at someone's effort to relax her by placing a smiley sticker directly in her vision; either way it hadn't worked. The claustrophobia crept over her like poison ivy. But 22 minutes and 31 seconds later it was done and the staff smiles sent her away with a reassurance of wellness to fumble back into her clothes.

Her cancer was eight years past and she was getting used to being around, each year she gained minimising her fear of its return, but now this bold black type screamed secondaries. Six to twelve month life expectancy at best... Googling for this information not one of her better ideas! At best? This wouldn't get her to Christmas, never mind to old age. And, reading down the remainder of her letter, three of these precious weeks were to be spent waiting on this test.

504 hours of her life later, Emma waited in a hospital bed for the doctors to say "you can go home tomorrow".

COMING HOME
by Marie Cunningham

She paces the floor, eagerly waiting for him to come home.
It's certainly been a long few days, of tears, sleepless nights and worrying is he alright?

Her mind drifts to memories of how her life has changed since the day he walked into it. From the start he'd certainly ruled her heart. He always made her laugh with his funny antics and strange little ways. Such as the cute way he ate his meals too quick, then would look at her with his gorgeous dark eyes and childish manner, as if to say, "I wish you hadn't let me do that."

He kept her up most nights too at the beginning, but she didn't mind not getting much sleep, she was just happy he was laid there next to her. Even though he snored!

She also loved how he'd wake her in the morning, by gently kissing her on the cheek, as if to say, "Come on then, let's have breakfast." Everything in her world seemed complete, 'til a few days ago when he hadn't come home after one of his nights out.

From day one she'd known he'd be a wanderer, but at first it didn't bother her, she even liked his free spirit, thought it was part of his appeal. But this was different, as he'd never not come home before.

Well, that was a lie! He'd stayed out all night before, but he'd always come home next day, usually with a smug look on his face to let her know he'd had a good night.

Where the hell was he?

He didn't even answer when she called!

The gut wrenching started by day two, as she knew something must be wrong. Had he been involved in a fight, or worse, been attacked? She'd rang local hospitals by day three, but no sign of him, although they said they would take note of his description and let her know if he turned up, but she knew they were just being kind to her.

She decided she would never give up hope that he'd turn up where he belonged, with her. Or maybe it was as simple as he'd found someone else to love him more?

No, that wasn't possible, as no one could love him more than she did.

But he might have found someone who gave him more attention; after all she'd been busy with her new job lately.

Suddenly her mobile rings. Her heart beats loudly as she answers it.

She closes the lid and sinks into the armchair. Then she starts to cry.

Thank God, he's on his way home.

She wipes her eyes on her sleeve, picks up a towel, blows her nose and heads for the front door. Her son James said he's got him.

The door opens and James walks in. He smiles as he hands Tubby over to her and she cradles him in her arms. He'd been found in someone's garden shed. That bloody cat!

DEAD END
by Johanna DeBiase

After returning from the tavern, where I was hiding out from heavy rains, I found my house at the bottom of the hill. I noted the tracks where the house slid through the mud and eyed the steep hillside. My body turned tense and laden. Since my husband ran away with my best friend's boyfriend, it was up to me to get the house back up the hill by myself. I surveyed the damage. The small cabin had cracking beams at its base and wood panels dangling on their last rusty nail. Otherwise, it showed remarkable resilience. The rope we used to pull it back up the hill the last three times was still intact. I had to make haste as the house was nearly in the road.

Grabbing the heavy rope with gloved hands, I began the Sisyphean climb. As I made my way up the hillside, I spotted Sammy's house above almost completely shaded in various pieces of yard junk, including several rusty old car carcasses, some tractor attachments, a couple of snowmobiles with their tracks settled deep into the mud, an old wood stove growing weeds out of the stout chimney pipe, a vintage travel trailer with windows busted out, and a couple of bikes without tyres. How come his shit never slid down the fucking hill? I kept my eyes down, better to keep pulling, keep climbing, not to see how much further still I had to go. Finally, I reached the plateau. One last heaving pull over the ledge to bring my cabin into its terraced place.

Inside, I put on the tea kettle and took off my gloves and muddy boots. Chrissy appeared at the open window.

"How ya' doin'?" she asked sweetly. She was new around here, not embittered enough to want to be left alone, still desperate enough to seek company. "Been rainin' pretty hard."

I poured hot water over the pine needles and rose hips I collected on my way home. "Just weather," I answered and fell to the couch, blowing strong air through puckered lips.

She was still outside peering in through the pane. The screen had fallen out long ago. The curtains needed to be rehung.

"We should leave here," she said, "everyone else has."

"Why should we do that?"

"Because... because we're meant to be happy and there's nothing here for anyone anymore."

"I'll never leave this place. I've got nowhere to go. This is my home." As if in response, the house let out an exhausted moan, settling back into its foundation.

10,000 PLAYMATES
(AFTER A VISIT TO TYNECOT CEMETERY)
by Brindley Hallam Dennis

Here, come closer, man. I tell you all about it, ey? They died in sight of this. Before my time, before yours too, I'd say. Have you got people here, ey? I played here when I was a boy. That's long ago too, man. We played war here too.

Het was so. We had ten thousand playmates, all under crosses row on row, ey? They're kept so clean, so tidy. All these flowers, the grass neatly mown, but it was these bunkers we came here to see, ey? As boys will. They had cleared them of the past by then, we thought. There were no bones, no skeletons. The spent shell cases had gone; the shrapnel splinters; the souvenirs. Only the concrete shell, it was like a skull itself, ey?

Even the biggest guns had not breached them. You see, these mere scratches, these flakes of concrete, down to the steel, but not through it. It is fifty metres, man, above the valley here, but then there were no trees left standing, not one brick upon another as far as you could see, yet still they came on, walking into the machine guns; Tommies, ANZACs, even black fellas, ey?

And now they lie here, in the foreign country. Het was much later when we came, in our corduroy short trousers and caps, crept in at the back. The entrance was not blocked up then. We imagined Fallschirmjagers, panzergrenadiers, and shot them too by the thousand with our wooden guns. I tell you, we meant no harm, man. We did what all boys do. You cannot see the gravestones from this slit, only the endless slope, down into the valley where their trenches were. We did not think of them, lying beneath the crosses, row on row, ey?

Then one night when the sun was low, we had already turned to go, and I looked back. The clouds had turned to flame as if the whole world burned outside. That's when he came, out of the darkness, silent as the past. His head was bandaged, ey? His tunic grey, like ash, his skin too, pale as death, his fingers bony. I was scared, man. My hair stood up, my legs shook, and the other boys were already gone, running across the short turf, between the rows of crosses, row on row, laughing into distance. But I stood here, inside, in darkness, with the sky on fire beyond the narrow opening, and he gripped my shoulder, turned me back to where his gun had rested. Bright bullets glinted in the ammunition belt, where we stood, he and I, while night came on, firing as he had fired before, until all were gone. After that they bricked the entrance up, lest other children entered and were lost.

Lean closer to the slit. Your shadow falls across my face. Lean closer, you feel my breath upon your cheek, ey?[1]

[1] *At Tynecot WW1 cemetery, near Ypres, the guide told us that the old bunkers had to be bricked up, to stop local children from playing war in them.*

46

TRUE CALLING
by Sharon Espeseth

Is teaching my true calling? I wondered. I generally did things the hard way. Instead of completing my education degree, I tried my wings after the minimum two years of university. Not realising my wings were still wet, I declined my parents' offer of help for my third, even fourth, year.

I planned to finish the remaining two years of my BEd through summer school and evening classes. I had not yet experienced the workload for a class of students. After two years of teaching and taking courses, I realised I was battling up a steep incline.

Seeking a different slope, I settled on a medical record librarian career – medical information intrigued me. In the 1960s, this course had been squeezed into a one-year program available in Regina, Saskatchewan.

My father drove me the 500 miles from Edmonton, Alberta. Arriving in Regina, we found a temporary rooming house. Dad returned home the next morning.

On Monday, I walked to the Regina General Hospital where I met my instructor, Mrs Lyndall, and our group of ten students. Ann, one of the students, told me she was getting reasonable room and board at the YWCA. I booked a room and moved my minimal belongings by taxi.

Considering myself a teaching dropout, I resolved to excel in this course, thus launching my new career. I threw my heart and mind into the challenge. I discovered I could ace the course. Top marks in high-school Latin helped with medical terminology and anatomy.

Recognising my motivation, Mrs. Lyndall groomed me for Canada-wide awards. Success in the course should guarantee me a good job, I figured. Besides attending church, a Sunday visit with Mom's cousins, and sharing walks and meals with my classmate, Ann, I studied.

I may have been homesick, but my achievements kept me going. Good reports allayed Mom and Dad's concerns about me. September, October, and November flipped right past me.

One morning in early December, I awoke dreading to go to the hospital. Carcinoma charts and studying illness sickened me. The hospital atmosphere suddenly nauseated me, and I realised my clothes were hanging loosely on my thinning body.

Mentally, I started re-living enjoyable moments with my third grade class, the relationships I had developed with my students and their parents, the camaraderie of my colleagues. Absence from teaching let me see its better side. Although teaching required preparation, marking, and report cards, it also offered the reward of seeing children learn and the joy of making learning fun.

On December 13, I called my family to say, "I'll be home tomorrow." Worried, my parents called my instructor. I caused an upset at home at both ends, but I confidently held my decision. Home before Christmas, I sent out resumés for three teaching positions, and I received three offers. I chose one.

In January, I was back home in the classroom, which became my domain for over thirty years. I survived teaching and I enjoyed my university studies. I have no regrets.

THE PAIN OF REMEMBERING
by Chris Foote-Wood

"Here you are, drink this," but Diane wasn't sure. Already deeply embarrassed, she wanted nothing more than to get away home. "It's alright, it's only water." The cheerful, middle-aged lady was smiling but insistent. Diane took the glass.

"Thank you." She drank quickly, gulping down the contents. "Thank you, thank you very much. I'll be alright now."

"Are you sure?" The elderly man with an air of authority had sat her down and told her to take deep breaths. "Are you sure you're alright?"

Diane nodded and handed back the almost empty glass. She took one more deep breath and stood up. "I'm alright. I'll be going home now."

"Are you sure?" he repeated. Diane tried to smile, but a smile would not come.

"Do you want someone to go with you?" It was the woman again.

"No, thank you all very, very much. I'm quite alright now." Diane pushed through the small crowd and walked away, firmly and quickly. She wasn't sure in which direction she was heading, but anything to get away from the small throng of well-wishers.

"She doesn't look well to me." "Someone should go with her." "Oh, let her go."

Soon Diane reached a corner, thankfully turning out of sight. She slowed, more deep breathing. The pain was still there, right under her heart. A few minutes ago, it had seemed like someone had slammed her in the midriff with a sledgehammer, making her double up. For the moment, her breathing had stopped. It didn't happen so often now, but anything could still set it off, a word, a sound or just a random thought forcing its unwanted way into her brain.

It was Michael. How she missed him! Ever since the policewoman had told her that Michael had been killed crossing the road, Diane had been staring into a bleak, black void. Time after time she punished herself with the same, pointless questions: "Why Michael? Why not me, Samantha, Richard? Why am I here and not him?" Guilty thoughts. The pain of remembering. But all she could remember were the last two words Michael had said to her on the phone the night before: "I'll be home tomorrow, just as always".

Fancy making a spectacle of herself in public! It must not, must not happen again. Nobody must know her guilty secret. There must be a way of breaking through. Focus, focus on something positive. What had the policewoman said? "Think of all the good times you had together, all the things he said to you."

"That's right," thought Diane. "What did Michael say? He'll be home tomorrow. Just as always." She smiled and walked on. Yes, Michael would be home tomorrow. Just as always.

THE POSTCARD
by Michael Foster

"I won't be in next week. I'm going home tomorrow."

That was what Barry had said a month ago. Julie hadn't thought much of his comment at the time. Now she couldn't get it out of her head.

Warming her hands on her cup of coffee, she stared out the rain soaked kitchen window at her garden. The grass was long and weeds were cropping up in the flowerbed. At eighty-one she was too old to maintain it herself. That was why three years ago she had employed a self-employed gardener named Barry Jones.

She took a seat at her rickety kitchen table. The house was quiet and had been since the death of her husband eight years ago. Her two sons never visited and she had very few friends. It was why she looked forward to Barry's visits once a week. After finishing work he would come in for a cup of tea and tell stories from his exciting life. He had never stayed in one place for long, joining the Army aged sixteen, leaving it ten years later to travel the world on a cruise ship, then returning to make his money gardening when he had been made redundant.

She grabbed the newspaper lying on the tabletop. It was five days old and she had read it cover to cover, but she could only venture to the newsagents for a new one when the weather was fine and with the aid of two walking sticks. She would have to go out at some point though as she was running out of food. If Barry was still here he would have bought some supplies for her.

Given his past, she knew she shouldn't have been surprised when he had disappeared. But the way he had completely vanished unnerved her. He didn't call her and her phone didn't even connect when she tried to call him. When she had visited his house two weeks ago she found it empty and abandoned. When her son had called her last week she had asked him to check Barry's website and he found it had been taken down. After saying he was going home, Barry had disappeared from the face of the earth.

She sighed and closed the crumpled newspaper, before slumping into her seat and listening to the rain beating against the window. She wondered what she could do today. She could barely face another day in front of the television watching Cash in the Attic, but there wasn't much else for her to do.

She heard the sound of the letterbox opening and shutting, and she slowly hoisted herself out of her seat and used her walking stick to shuffle to the hallway. Only one letter was waiting for her on the mat, a postcard depicting a Cornish fishing village. She recognised the handwriting immediately and, her spirits lifting, she started reading. The message began, "Dear Julie, I'm home now…"

LIFE CHANGES
by Alwyn Frankland

Paul's head pounded as he strode along the mud baked path. He was going home tomorrow, but his mind was still in turmoil; running away hadn't solved anything. But what was he going back to? What would home be from now on? The pungent smell of baby puke and sleepless nights.

His home had always been his sanctuary, a place to chill out and feel safe (although at seventeen he would never have admitted this to anyone). Now he felt scared – his whole life was going to change. I'm not ready for this, he thought. Dad told me I had to deal with it like a man, but I don't feel like a man – all I want is for things to go back to how they were.

It felt as if his whole world was crashing down around him. He'd only just started dating Amy – she was in his year at school. They were taking the same A-level subjects and teamed up with the notion that two heads were better than one. He felt himself blushing at the thought of some of their so-called study sessions.

A sudden stab of panic shot through his body. Oh God, he thought, how am I going to tell my friends – I'll just die of embarrassment. Jeez! I suppose Friday nights will have to stop? Friday night was when his friends came round to chill and listen to music and play on his games console or Wii. He was always the first in the group to have the latest games and equipment; his Mum always said he was indulged rather than spoilt.

"Hi Paul, how's your Gran?" A man's voice snapped him out of his deliberations and he realised that he had come to the end of the path and was approaching the village green.

"She's fine Charlie, thanks for asking." Although he remembered that she was anything but fine when he arrived on her front doorstep feeling very sorry for himself. His Dad had already called her to say he had walked out. Paul's Gran doted on him, so he hadn't been prepared for her reaction. She tartly told him to stop being so selfish and remember that his wasn't the only life that would change. A new baby was something to be loved and cherished – not resented. In his heart he knew that she was right and that was why she was making him go home tomorrow and face up to reality. Paul began to feel guilty – he knew he had behaved badly, so he pulled his BlackBerry from his pocket, pressed the required buttons and waited. His Father answered.

"Dad, I'm sorry about my reaction when you and Mum broke the news. It's just I've been an only child for so long it'll take a bit of getting used to the idea of having a baby brother or sister around. Can you pick me up from the station tomorrow? I'm coming home."

THE CARAVAN
by Ben Frew

By the time the sun hit its apogee, the caravan I was travelling with had slowed to a crawl. The shadows had contracted into the space of each new footprint, and salted beads of sweat dissolved on impact on the scorched sand.

Keffou, the guide, had taken to whipping his mules incessantly, drawing shrieks of dissent from some of the more sensitive women and children. The animals themselves – mules laden with Arabic cloth and Persian grain; camels carrying the obese, wealthy tourists – lolloped hypnotically in metronomic rhythm, panting with bone-dry tongues and flared nostrils. It was hard, though, for the Europeans to feel pity. They had paid well to be taken across the desert, and were too engrossed in their own distress and exhaustion to sympathise with the ill-treated beasts of burden. Besides, the whip-crack kept them awake; strengthened their focus and fortified their resolve.

One traveller, an Italian wool merchant famed in Genoa for the vitality of his dyes, suffered from hallucinations and heatstroke, often screaming vulgarities into the unblemished sky. "Whore!" he swore violently. "Bastardo!"

Beside him, his wife motioned the sign of the cross, pleading divine forgiveness for her husband's indiscretions. All the while the guides stared steadfastly forwards, unable to translate the blasphemes that pulsed in their ears.

It was not until the shadows began to grow again that Lombardi ceased his caterwauling, replacing curses for tears and shaking his balding sunburnt head, which had, by then, slumped downwards into the cavity between his chest and gut.

At the rear of the pack, Myanmia's blind children held hands and moved in time to the sound of whipped leather and torn animal skin. Their mother, a graceful Bedouin wrapped in red and azure silken robes, carried their only surviving lamb on her shoulders, its bleat dulled to bare breath. Occasionally she would reveal a flask from beneath her clothes and nurse the tiny retiring animal with the few drops of water she had maintained. Keffou had insisted from the outset that no water would be spared for the animals, and Myanmia had necessarily refined her surreptitious feeding into a fine art. Try as she would to keep it alive, the lamb would not survive the journey.

By the time Myanmia succumbed to the inevitable and laid the lamb's carcass on the burning sand, a smile began to curl into Keffou's dry, cracked lips. He had felt the ground grow firmer beneath his feet, and had tasted a gathering moisture on the steady southern breeze. He could hear, rising up from the valley that now dropped down before him, the distant echo of song and syncopated drumbeat. And with all of his sharpened senses pricked, he knew that the group had made it.

"Home tomorrow," he bellowed to the grateful gatherers behind him. And as the valley's welcoming reflection was painted on his smiling eyes, he drew blood from the ass's ass with his most enthusiastic whip yet.

HOME TOMORROW
by Susan Giles

Annie sends her husband home with a firm shove and warm smile, as fed-up of his presence as he must be of hers. "I will be fine," she promises, "and so will Rose; just like Doctor Young said." Tom pretends he want to stay, that another night with the two of them squeezed into her hospital bed won't be the last straw for his sciatica, but Annie won't take no for an answer. He gives her one last pleading smile as he passes through the door, and she replies with a jaunty wave, her gaze already slipping to the cot at the foot of her bed.

She counts to ten before clambering out, creeping down towards it. She knows she shouldn't, knows that tomorrow is a big day and that baby Rose should be allowed as much sleep as possible, but the pull is magnetic. She feels a thrill as she peers over the edge of the cot, identifies the dusky pink of her daughter's skin against the pale candy coloured blanket, the silk-edged hat with its tiny embroidered rose. The perfect gift, her mother-in-law suggested, for a perfect baby girl.

Annie reaches out, tweaks the hat, thinking it's too big, too uncomfortable and she wishes she could take it off without stirring her. Wishes she'd stood her ground when her husband placed it on Rose's head, covering the fluff of dark hair, insisting that it fitted, looked too cute to remove. Rose had been in his arms then, her blanket suddenly harsh against the white of his shirt, and Annie's arms had ached with the absence. She'd crossed them over her chest, folded her hands in her lap, finally started stroking the velvet rabbit tucked into the cot just for something to do, and when it was time to return Rose to the cot, when the rhythmic snuffle of her breath suggested sleep, Annie had been the one to lay her down and tuck her in. She should have taken the hat off then.

But she didn't and now it is still on poor Rose's head, gaping, a scrap of skin visible beneath the material. It might fall off in the night, might get twisted behind her head or caught in her mouth. These and a hundred other possibilities flicker through Annie's mind, and her hands reach out and, gently, so gently, remove the hat. That's better, she thinks, straightening the blanket again, much safer. She throws the unwanted hat towards the end of the bed, doesn't see where it lands, and reaches a finger to stroke the air above Rose's cheek.

She knows now it is her turn to sleep, to curl up in her bed so that tomorrow will come quicker; so she can introduce Rose to the world proper, show her off to the waiting faces, and accept their cooing compliments. Knows that she should sleep, but doesn't. Sits instead on the end of the bed, and watches her daughter as the hours roll on.

SOUNDS PERFECT, RIGHT?
by Hannah Glancey

Everything was always happening in the future, never right now. You'd kind of forget about today in anticipation of tomorrow. Today would fade, you'd be careless with it. Let it fly off with the wind. You'd watch it swirl away on the currents, tipping past houses, shops, suburbs, fields 'til it was in a country it no longer knew.

So there I was, sat on a train, contemplating tomorrow and making my way across country, head lightly resting on the glass. And, I thought, it's not long now. My iPod was playing The Smiths. 'Good times for a change', Morrissey sang as the green blur of fields went by. A smile grew upon my lips; I could see it reflected on the window. I laughed. To no one in particular, just to myself. I was having a day, one where everything was good. I was nearly there, I was nearly home. It had been so long, three months at least, but then three days is an age when you are young.

The remains of my train shop sandwich sat in front of me, the taste of damp cardboard permeating my mouth. It's true when they say how it's funny the things you remember. Yet, that day, nothing was going to bring me down. Tomorrow felt closer than it had ever been. The first thing I decided I was going to do was make the best poached eggs in the world. Then a bath. Then a crap film. Then the pub. Sounds perfect, right?

I opened a can of beer, may as well get in the mood now, relax a little, I remember thinking. No rush, no hurry, just nothing. All I registered was how many stops were left 'til mine. Three.

At the second to last stop, he got on. One stop away, one can of beer left. Would I have been quicker sober? It really was the last leg. I was so preoccupied I didn't even notice him sit next to me. I couldn't tell you anything about him, even now. By the time

I noticed him was by the time anyone noticed him and, to be fair, that was when it was the clichéd "too late".

I don't want to talk about it anymore. I don't want to remember. All I can say is it really is something when a plate of glass shatters right by your face.

Today would be gone before you knew. You'd wonder then why you ever wasted it. You'd justify it with the excitement of tomorrow, but would you ever question what if? What if tomorrow never came?

PLAYING WITH FIRE
by Carole Green

The secret of juggling and eating fire is this: you must be prepared to enjoy the agony of a constantly scalded gullet and hands. It is a mundane mystery, but one which not everyone can endure. On his 38th birthday when dragged along reluctantly to see a fiery sideshow, he realised as he watched, that this was his medium; the very essence of his nature. It was something he'd been doing all his life since the first grade when he shared his boiled sweets with Angela and kissed her damp lips, and then later stopped to kiss her sister, also on the long walk home that afternoon. And as a young man he was sincerely indecisive, genuinely unable to choose between the many women he kept on the boil – loving them intensely the moment he was with them, his ardour cooling as they were swallowed up in the banalities of tidying, studying, working, cooking, raising children.

After that fateful birthday he quit his 9-5 and spent his days sleeping and nights as part of an ensemble swallowing not only fire but coals, brimstone, melted beer glasses. And then he met Ashley who accidentally spilt vodka down his chest whilst watching his fire juggling act, setting him ablaze and leaving him with third degree burns and a baby smooth torso. She was the clumsiest person he'd ever encountered; knocking the drip stand over when she visited him next day in the hospital, getting her foot caught in the low wastepaper bin by the door, dropping his cellphone down the loo when she borrowed it to call a friend and tell her of the disaster and the gorgeous man she'd almost killed.

He was smitten. Twelve years later he was still juggling: laundry, cooking, three children, two rabbits, home renovation, a medium-sized dog – the only thing never up in the air was his devotion to Ashley. She continued ineptly shedding and misplacing things: weight, jobs, friends, until distractedly she crushed their life one night when she lost control of the steering wheel while bending to retrieve a fallen earring. There was only one word left to describe this new pain he felt: incandescent.

THE BOY AT THE WINDOW
by She Harris

She'll be through in a minute. I shouldn't have listened in, I know, but when the phone rang I knew it would be him. I didn't speak, but they'll have heard the click.

I'd been waiting by the window for hours. Absolutely hours. She'd have made something up if I hadn't heard. There's something wrong. I know there is. Like with Jonno's Mam and Dad. They're divorced now.

"Can't get off the rig," he said. My Dad's a diver. Somebody told me it's a very dangerous job. But my Dad knows what he's doing, so there's no need for me to worry.

"The weather," he said. Mam didn't believe him.

We watched the weather forecast last night. Mam said he'd be home this time. He's been away for absolutely ages.

So now she's on the phone to Mike across the road. I know it's Mam he's talking to, 'cos he turned away from me. That's when I knocked the glass of Ribena over. There'll be hell to pay when she gets through here, 'cos it won't come out of the carpet. Or my pyjamas for that matter. Whatever.

Sometimes I wish that Mike was my Dad. At least he lives close enough to see me every day. And he has a dog. A red setter. Bracken he calls her. She's warm and silky and licks me. He lends me books as well. Ones he's had since he was my age. Beano and Dandy annuals mostly, from the 1980s. He's written his name in the front of them. 'This book belongs to – Michael Storey.' Then there's an address where he must have lived when he was a kid.

I'd better get up out of this corner. I'll move the phone out of the mess on the table where I spilt the Ribena. Then I'll go into the kitchen to find a cloth and Mam will cover the mouthpiece of the phone and say, "All right, son?" She'll tell me that Dad's very busy and very very sorry. I'll nod and smile to show her that I'm not bothered. She'll say, "I'll be through in a minute." She'll follow me back into the other room and she'll make a clicking noise with her tongue when she sees the Ribena. She'll probably tell me off. Then she'll move the table into the middle of the room and I'll turn the chair so that its back faces the window. She'll tell me it's time for bed and, when she thinks that I'm not looking, she'll wave to Mike.

Later he'll be round tapping softly on the door. I'll hear glasses clinking and they'll be talking and laughing and I'll get under the quilt and pretend that, when I wake up, I'll look out of the window and see Dad walk up the road with his case and bags. He'll wave to me and I'll be shouting, "Mam, Mam! It's Dad! He's home."

HOME TOMORROW
by Jennifer Harrison

L ily took a sip of bitter coffee from the chipped mug that had been irreverently slung in front of her and reflected that, although she'd come on this trip hoping for an epiphany, she certainly hadn't expected one to come along and hit her in the face in the slightly insalubrious surroundings of a rundown pavement café on a dusty side street in Buenos Aires.

Not that she wasn't grateful for the epiphany finally arriving, she acknowledged sagely, smoothing back her unruly blonde hair. After all, the gaining of a little inner wisdom had been an important factor in her decision to wander solo around South America for many months, her only company a bumper tube of sunscreen and a litany of dire warnings to beware the gangs of semi-feral, guacamole-guzzling bandits who, her family had been certain, would mug, murder or sell her as a slave the moment her plane touched down on Latin soil. But she'd thought profundity, if it was going to strike, would have done so somewhere inspirational, perhaps at the breathtaking Iguazu Falls she'd visited on the Argentinean border some weeks ago, or the beautiful El Doradillo beach, where she'd had the unforgettable experience of watching carefree whales bask in the frothy waters of the Atlantic ocean. Not, she mused with a snort, at a grim café sporting grubby plastic tables and menus curling at the corners.

A peal of throaty laughter interrupted her wandering thoughts, reminding Lily that it wasn't, in fact, her surroundings per se that were responsible for her newly-gained wisdom. She snapped her eyes to the source of the laughter, a group of vivid young women occupying the table next to her, and acknowledged with a wry nod that it was actually the presence of these exotic porteñas which had sent her thoughts fluttering along their current pathway to self-awareness. She set her coffee down on the stained table top and stared at them; a group of carefree friends, dark eyes flashing with vivacity, life and – well, happiness, Lily thought enviously. They were clearly a close-knit bunch, conversing easily in colourful Spanish, hands gesturing animatedly, their chatter interspersed with bouts of unrestrained giggles.

As she continued to gaze at them, the hot sun beating down on her sticky skin, Lily finally realised the full irony of her situation.

She'd travelled half way across the world to Find Herself; and five months' later, she'd done exactly that. She'd Found Herself alone in a strange city, desperately missing the friends and family she'd abandoned back in the UK. Her trip had been a glamorous adventure. But what she truly wanted was what these young women had; she wanted to be surrounded by the people she loved. Nothing mattered to her more.

She glanced down at her watch, suddenly rendered impatient by her new insight.

There was time.

If she left now, she could be on a flight by tonight.

The thought made her smile.

By tomorrow, she would be home. Back where she belonged.

POISON TOAD
by Lewis Harrison

H e'd never seen a toad in real life, before he was blown up, but that's what it had looked like to him.

He remembered looking up toward the sky from the field where he'd thrown himself. His vision almost whited out by the blistering morning light. He remembered glimpsing a black speck rising through the carmine sun, steadily growing larger. Watching it cut through the air and thinking it was an almost beautiful thing. There hadn't been time to run.

It didn't roll like he'd expected it to. The grenade just landed with a thump amongst the corn and sat there like a toad of some sort, waiting to see what he'd do next.

•

As a child growing up in Northallerton, he would sit in front of the television watching nature programmes for hours. Most Sunday afternoons were spent curled up on the sofa watching The Natural World, sometimes with his mother, sometimes not.

Often he would think he'd like to walk in the footsteps of his hero, the show's narrator David Attenborough. He imagined stalking through the jungles of South America or the mountains of Asia, searching for a herd of elk or a glimpse of an elusive mountain lion. It seemed an exciting way to spend one's life. Though in the end he followed in his father's boot-prints and joined the Royal Marines.

One of these Sundays the show featured the cane toad – or the poison toad, as it is also known. They were small, warty creatures armed with a poison strong enough to kill a human. The programme said the cane toad had spread like an illness across Australia since being introduced to the country as a pest controller in the 1940s. Now it was killing off native predators such as dingos, monitor lizards and crocodiles with its venom. Contained in glands on its back, the poison caused rapid heartbeats, convulsions and paralysis.

•

From his bed in the field hospital the man thinks of all of these things.

He thinks back to the fruitless dawn patrol. Of their return. Of the fear he felt when the Taliban ambushed. The adrenaline swelling his veins. Diving for cover amongst the maize.

He remembers dragging his sweat-soaked body across the mud and laying flat on top of the grenade with his back to it. Hoping his backpack would be enough to save his life and those of his friends. Not knowing the force of that blast would be the last sensation he would feel.

Most of all, though, he thinks back to those times at home. Those hours spent lying on the sofa with the afternoon sunlight streaming through the windows and playing across the living room walls. Watching incredible creatures in exotic, foreign lands. He thinks of those times and he wishes himself back there, back home. He hopes he'll see those wonders again.

HOME TOMORROW
by Barbara Haswell

"Hurry up Jack. The taxi will be here any minute."

"Can't be arsed. She might not be there anyway. She's a slag! What Mam puts her kids in care?"

"She's not what you think, she's your Mam and she loves you. She's just had a rough time. The social worker is helping her to get sorted, turn herself around."

"Those idiots! Hate them, took us away, even put our dog in some place that's crap. Anyways you get paid for me. If me Mam did, we'd still be together. She could pay the rent, the leccy would be on, and we'd eat every day. She could buy us all the gear – trainers, trackies, the lot. You lot just have kids for the money, have a tidy house when the social workers come, kit us out. Me Mam could foster, if she hadn't got that... what's it called when you've been nicked? Nicked for shoplifting in Asda, she had no money, what else could she do?"

"Let's have a look at you. What a smart lad, your Mam will think you're cool."

"If she comes. She doesn't like them social workers sitting in on our time together. It's gross – you can't be normal like."

"They're just wanting things to be right for you both."

"Git nebby you mean."

"Have some breakfast pet, it's a long ride."

"Aye miles from me Mam's. They should put you near your mates, your school, if you go that is. They're mental."

"I was the nearest foster carer. It's not that they wanted you to be so far away."

"The kids around here are git weird, not the sort I hang around with. Can you wrap that bacon bun up for me Mam? She'll be hungry."

"Course I can, and what about this box of chocolates Dave

bought me? Take them too."

"Thanks. It's just well... it's not like being with your own. It's strange like, everyone knows you don't belong – that you're a foster kid. They ask you dead private things like, where's your Dad? What fucking Dad? Never had one. How do you cope with that? I'm going back to bed, life's shit when you're 13 and no one gives a fart!"

"Come on Jack. Your Mam wants to see you and you mustn't let her down. It'll be okay. Have a good time. I'll do your favourite for tea – mince and dumplings."

"Shove it up your arse! I hate you and your shite food!"

Four hours later...

"Well looks like all went well, what did I tell you?"

"Mince and dumplings. Fantastic! My last meal here. You know what? They held a meeting, with me and me Mam, and it's all decided, I'm going home tomorrow. How great is that!"

"That's fantastic. As my Mam used to say, there's no place like home. I'm really glad it's all worked out."

"Thanks. You're mint. After me Mam that is!"

NEVER LOOK BACK
by Sarah Henderson

inally I escaped the town I named 'Boxton', my suffocating prison for seeming eternity. Pastures new offered shiny dreams and journalism college. Striding into college on the first day, my jet black biker boots carried my zipped up confidence. I couldn't believe my luck when I mét Peter. His accidentally retro look and manly features inspired me to think I'd met the man to build a family with. Even two months down the line when he pissed the bed and endlessly played his only CD, 'Evergreen' by Will Young. My home was perfectly etched, I'd rub out any mistakes if they appeared. Peter, me and Sonny now a pebble in my stomach would be my perfect picture.

Startled by the speed of events, my 'Boxton' family started to sound nervous and encouraged me to pay a visit. I quashed all their concerns, my home was here and I eagerly awaited Sonny's arrival. We painted his room daffodil yellow, he would be my little ray of sunshine. I fell in love with this future whilst a sultry brown temptation wearing nothing but glass drew Peter into her raptures.

The next few months Peter slept on wet sofas as his liquid dominatrix ran loose in his mind and body. His empty promises soaked in ever sweetening deceit. Pushing this aside, as when Sonny arrived Peter's metamorphosis would begin; parenting often brings out responsibility.

Sliding down the hospital bed like a lightning bolt, Sonny was born. Cradling him while Lakeland blue eyes blinked up at me, I was mesmerised. Peter's mother dragged him from the arms of the King's Head to see us. "I was wetting the baby's head," he slurred. "You've got to celebrate with your mates, aint ya?" he tried to pick Sonny up and was deafened by ear splitting cries.

The only certainty we have is change; people change, don't they? I began to see Peter's drinking as an intruder, a monster with talons who could kill yet entice. I turned into a wailing banshee and tried to make him leave his home full of taps. He laughed when I was banned from his "residence"; he was welcomed there as part of their lives, a piece of their furniture.

Later as he crashed into the cot like a boat at sea crashing into rocks, instinct took over to save Sonny. I pushed him away and he fell like a great giant felled, now in a huddle and falling into slumber. Sonny slept soundly by my side that night, unaware his tiny body was nearly crushed by his father. I stayed awake all night, alert for further danger. An early morning knock at my bedroom door had me leaping out of bed like a wildcat. Peter appeared, cup of tea in hand. As I drove away that day I was glad I'd texted my friend last night: "Coming home tomorrow". I'd see her soon; she'd be at the motorway stop to meet me.

NUMBER 65
by Helen Holmes

I wish I'd a tenner for every time I've been asked what I think about on "the lonely walk". I'd be a rich man. "Think" is the wrong word, for starters. I'm doin' the job I trained to do. Like a plumber or a car mechanic or an electrician. You're programmed. You crack on. Ticker's going like the bleedin' clappers. Course it is. Anyone who tells you different's a liar. Adrenaline makes you antsy. That's the point of it. Eyes out on stalks. Ears flappin'. Back of yer neck goosey. You an' the lads need to get yer arses out of there. Pronto. You're sittin' ducks. This voice keeps yammerin' in yer 'ead: "Get the fuck outta there!" Your voice. Sun's turned traitor, too. Bastard's barbecuin' yer brains. Yer mitts are all slimy. You wipe yer palms on the seat of yer trousers. Dust tickles yer throat. You try to swallow. No deal. No spit. But lose yer cool and you're all dead meat. You take deep breaths, put one foot in front of the other. Not too fast… twenty-seven… not too slow… twenty-eight… nice an' even… twenty-nine… gently does it… thirty.

There's a picture of Ellie an' Morag in the space behind me eyes. The photie's in me breast pocket, all scrunched up an' faded. Must gerra new one. Last summer in the garden. Ellie an' Morag squintin' into the sun. On the seat under that poncy "pergola" Ellie kept bangin' on about. The spit of each other. Peas in a pod, my girls. They're really laughin', not just gurnin' at the camera. Can't remember what was funny now. "Time to come home now, Daddy," Morag says on the phone last night. Too bloody right, sweet'eart. Well time. She's growin' up that fast.

Sixty-four, I've done, this tour. In five months. Broken the back of it, any rate, so I'll only 'ave a short stint to do when I get back. That's worth bein' knackered for.

This one's the sixth today. You never know what to expect from these little prickteasers. No two alike, nowadays. You gorra suss 'em out straight away. No second chances. An extra wire tucked underneath, mebbe? Or a second trigger lurkin' under a stone? Last week, one 'ad a dollar bill glued to the pressure plate. Ha bloody ha.

Steve was for callin' it quits 'alf an hour back, but I says nah, let's press on, finish the job, else you'll be trailin' back in the mornin'.

"Yeah, s'all right for some lucky bastards," Steve says, "buggering off home tomorrow."

I can feel 'im an' the other lads watchin' as I pull the little brush out of me pocket. I kneel down, stretch out on the bakin' ground. Me buckle's diggin' into me belly. I shift onto me side. I can touch the metal casin' with me fingertips. Wotcher, number 65, what makes you tick then? Let's brush some of this crap off yer face, shall we?

SNOW BLIND
by Kevin Horsley

I am outside having a cigarette, walking to stretch my aching limbs when, through the heavy snowfall, a disembodied black tie approaches. The tie becomes a white suit complemented with a white fedora placed atop a smiling Mediterranean face.

He tells me not to panic and we will soon be home; his voice has an exoticism to it that I cannot place.

Before I can reply, he takes his gleaming smile to the other passengers who appear to float like shadows in the whiteout.

I shiver as I exhale and watch the people milling around in the distance. The heat of the cigarette is a single point of burning intensity against my lips and I know it is nearly done so I drop it, pull my hood tight and hug myself to keep warm.

Taking out my phone from my jacket pocket, I call Janet.

I need to tell her I will not be home until tomorrow and how sorry I am to be missing the party. Of all the days for this to happen it had to be her parents' fortieth wedding anniversary.

All I get is static.

Frustrated, I type out a text of apology instead. At least this will send when I get a signal. I know in advance she will not be happy about this, but I am resigned to the facts and have at least avoided an unfortunate argument.

The thought of confrontation tempts me to have another smoke but there is one left and something tells me I will need it later.

The other people are wandering like lost souls. A few of them have congregated into groups, but most of them are standing solitary figures doing similar activities to me. One or two are huddled on the ground and look like refuse sacks waiting to be collected.

My eyes view the train, the long black phallic engine with several carriages attached. It stands motionless on the tracks, behind it are barren trees coated with a dusting of snow; if I was not so cold

I could appreciate the picturesque Christmas card scene a little more.

Climbing aboard, I find a steward in the aisle. He directs me to my seat and mumbles that no one knows what has happened yet but it is being investigated.

I do not realise how tired I am and slip into peaceful slumber soon after I sit down.

A loud thunderclap shocks me awake and I shudder involuntarily.

The man in the white suit returns, still smiling. "It is time," he says in his distinct accent and points to the door.

I make my way back outside and see shimmering doorways appear. The other passengers walk through them and disappear into the brightness, a thunderclap resonates through the air with each occurrence.

Finally I understand. I drop my phone into the snow and smoke my final cigarette, then make my way towards the bright outline of a doorway and know I will never return home again.

HOME TOMORROW
by Leo Howes

The world changed on the 20th of June, not that anyone but a handful of people noticed the change. It didn't make the news; the world didn't change with a bang or a flash but with a whimper, an almost silent change that could have been disguised by the breathing of a mouse. The world didn't change for everyone but it changed for me in the blink of an eye. I'd just bought a handmade suit, top of the line, cost me an arm and a leg. I didn't expect to be wearing it so soon but needs must. There's nothing like the feel of a new shirt straight out of the packet, ironed so there are no creases. I don't usually wear a shirt during the day but today it's a special occasion. The man who helped me in to it was all smiles.

"The ladies will love you in this," he said. Smoothing down the front, he grinned at me. "What's the occasion? Wedding? Anniversary?"

I stay quiet, looking him in the eye with a half smile on my face like I'm posing for a passport photograph.

"The strong silent type, eh?" Lighting a cigarette, he offered me one. "No? Well, I can't blame you. These things will kill ya. I'll be right back with your trousers." He walks out the back laughing, leaving me alone in the shop. It's freezing in here. I wish they would turn up the heating but if that's the way these guys work, who am I to complain?

"Nice suit. This must have cost a fortune. Looks as if it's my size. If I thought I could get away with it, I'd keep this and give you one of mine. Who would know? Well, apart from you." He fingered the fabric. "How did you afford something like this? You must be making a week what I make in a month."

Being helped into my shirt was one thing, but my trousers – that is a sensation I wasn't used to. As soon as I was suited and booted I was on my way. It was years since I'd seen my family. Mam and Dad were still living in the same small town where I was born, although the house I grew up in was gone, knocked down and rebuilt for modern housing. I hadn't seen it but I heard that they had squeezed three houses on the plot of land where we used to have our house and garden. Those things must be tiny. It's going to be quite the reunion. My friends are making their way from all over just to see me. My sister will be there with her husband and my niece; she'll be, what, ten now. There'll be all kinds of stories told, even some that shouldn't – the memories of a lifetime. Then I'll say goodbye to them all when they screw the lid of my coffin down. Well, it won't be long now; I'll be home tomorrow.

WORDS
by John Hoyland

"That's, four, five, eight, and nine and double it to eighteen." John looking pleased with his first word on his trusty old travel Scrabble. Sue glanced at him sideways and squeezed out a reluctant, "Sssssss, all right." The word 'HOME' was staring at her. With no vowels on her own rack she put an 'R' and a 'W' above and below the 'O' to make the word 'ROW'.

"Sixsssss," purred Sue, as she wrote down the score.

After a long pause, John finally linked up 'TOMOR' with 'ROW' to make 'TOMORROW'.

"That's thirteen, babe."

"Good one, baby."

John was already plundering the small cloth tile bag as her words drifted over him. She looked at her tile rack then at the two words on the small magnetic board. It suddenly struck her that the words 'HOME' and 'TOMORROW' were exactly what they would be doing in the morning, as they had to leave "The Road Kill Arms" as John had nicknamed their B&B. A wave of sadness fell over Sue.

"I've got a cry stuck, baby," fell out of Sue's mouth.

John, who was deep in thought trying to form a word that included his 'X' on a triple said, "Eh!" He looked up from his tile rack to see Sue's face collapsing into sadness. He put his rack down on the over-washed duvet cover, reached over, and put his arm around her as one of the mattress springs twanged. "Ah, babe, what's up?"

Sue spoke in her little girl voice. "I don't want to go home tomorrow, baby."

"We have to babe, it's time to go. Anyway that stoat kebab we had last night was a novelty but I wouldn't like it every week!"

"Oh no, not Colin!"

Sue snuggled her face into John's upper torso. They had both seen a stoat the day before, running along a riverbank. It was a stunningly white, bouncy creature that Sue had straight away christened, Colin.

"No, it was probably Colin's father. It was a bit tough on the old gnashers that one," said John.

"Noooooo," said Sue, as her feet and legs did a little tap and shuffle. The funnies were not helping, thought John. She raised her head and looked at him with her big brown cow eyes. John tinkered with her hair and said, "You know we have to go, babe," then drew her back into his body. It had been a lovely two-day break for them both, hiking, laughing, and loving. It was only their second break away from their hometown in the short time they had been together. She had been excited that she could finally tick off one of the things on her own Bucket List. Locating the cottage used by the signalman in one of her favourite films, 'The Railway Children', was something she would never forget. Even at forty-nine she was still a little girl at heart. A child. A dreamer.

HOME TOMORROW
by Anthony Hulse

As I sit in my wheelchair and gaze through the patio doors towards my garden, I purposely ignore my hideous reflection. I inhale my petrol-drenched body, the match between my ravaged fingers about to release me from my misery and suffering. I feel the tears streaming down my deformed face, and think back to that fateful day in Basra.

Corporal Daley constantly reminded me that we were to return home tomorrow. Little did I know that those haunting words would later come back to haunt me; spoken not by my comrade, but my wife of five years.

We watched the demonstration from the safety of our Warrior tank. We expected no trouble, but it was obvious that the Iraqi demonstrators were becoming hostile towards us. Bricks were now being thrown, and one such missile shattered our viewing sight. We now had no choice but to open the hatch, an action that would condemn me to my fate.

I heard the petrol bomb smashing beside me, before I realised that the flames were now licking at my torso. The screaming and the reek of petrol, I remember well, but it was the agonising burning of my skin that prompted me to leave our haven. I leapt from the tank and rolled on the ground, my entire body, including my face and hair, now ablaze. I remember the mob cheering, before my comrades came to my aid.

After several skin grafts, my body now functions, but my disfigurement prevents me from venturing outdoors. The nightmares will not go away and, having ample time to ponder over my pathetic existence, I sometimes think that I was fated to die in that blazing coffin. Fate is something that I always believed in, and my saviours had surely altered the course of mine.

My disfigurement and my confinement to my wheelchair, I could possibly tolerate, but the absence of my wife, Ann, I cannot. After I was released from the burns unit, I could see that her smile was false, her giveaway eyes unable to disguise the resentment that she had for my grotesqueness. It was understandable when she left me for her lover, who could offer her psychical love, and not just words.

It has been three weeks now since she walked out the door to visit her sister. Her words were similar to those uttered by Corporal Daley, so long ago. "My sister is ill, John, but I'll return home tomorrow."

Visits from my friends are now non-existent, and I have not even received a call from Ann. Food is of no concern to me, for my ravaged body is now undernourished.

I stare into my garden, the radiant sunshine unable to summon me outdoors. I look down at the match; the match that will eventually release me from my suffering. I strike the match, and utter the words, "home tomorrow". I feel no pain, as the flames ignite my desolate body. I will soon be at peace; my fate predetermined.

HOME TOMORROW: WANDERING
by Catherine Hume

Wandering, always wandering.

For a moment, for weeks, even for months, I rest, I stay, I am content. Each time that I have rested for too long, basking in the evening summer sun, someone would come and kick the sun lounger from beneath me, and they would stare at me in shadow, covering me with their darkness until I bundle up my belongings and leave. It always happens like this.

It happened like this two months ago. Two months ago, I was in the street, my face streaming, and those good people said they'd help me. Two nights ago, I heard their hearts break with platitudes, but they didn't give me a home. They waved me off, having done their bit, and that's me and my bundle again, wandering.

I know where I could stay. There are people who would welcome me with open arms. I know who they are, and I could go back to them and be like them again, be one of them again, but I don't want to. Part of me does, of course. Part of me knows there is a place for me among perverts and murderers, but I don't want to become like them again. Part of me knows there is a place for me among the hypocrites who stab their own hearts for everyone to see the blood flowing, but I don't want to become their project again. And so I wander.

I would like to live among the nice people – people who have nice children and nice holidays on Greek islands, who sponsor nice children in the third world. I'd like to live among them, but I know I'm not like them. I could pretend for a while, but after the veil is stripped away, an accident in conversation over an espresso, tipping the black, tainting them, I am revealed. They will see that I am not like them, and they will tolerate me, making the strain obvious, until I do the decent thing and leave.

And so I wander, never finding a place to rest, never finding a place to call home, until the day when I will finally fall on my knees, hearing the one voice I want to hear. I don't know when that day will come, so I will wander, knowing that my journey is already mapped out ahead of me. It's a long and lonely journey, and I do wonder if I can go on like this, though I am always looking upwards, to the sunrise, to tomorrow.

HOME TOMORROW
by Tracey Iceton

He's coming home tomorrow.

He's a tiny pink bundle, an armful of warmth. I could carry him home in my pocket. His star-fish hand reaches out and grips a lock of my hair, strangles it tight. I clutch him to me. Kiss his wet, gummy mouth. Give him a finger to suck on. Dreams of his life flood my world, quenching the parched landscape.

He's in his uniform. The first he'll wear; navy blazer, grey shorts, white shirt, striped tie. I sent him out early, neatly tucked and fastened. He's home late, wrinkled and messy. He smiles, laughs. I prayed all day for that smile, that laugh. Expected a pout on his perfectly red mouth, dreaded tears. I swoop him up into my arms.

He rushes to the table. Leaves his skateboard, muddy gritted wheels, on the kitchen floor. Don't leave it there. I'm going out again after tea. He swallows the mound of mash in two mouthfuls. Some of it smears around his mouth. I grab a tissue and clear the gunk so I can see his smile. Don't, Mum. I'm not a baby. Yes you are.

He wakes me with the front door. I was listening for it anyway. Footsteps heavy and sodden with lager on the stairs. His gurgled choking, the flushing of the toilet. I get up to help. He leans on the doorframe, swaying in an imaginary breeze. His lips move in slow-motion. The words are slurred. I help him to bed.

He waves the paper triumphantly. It's the first thing I see, after his radiant grin, brighter than June sun. He passed. With honours. The tight-jawed, pursed-lipped, chewed-biro nights were not for nothing. I steal a hug. No kiss now, he's too old. A man. All grown up and ready to go.

He brings Jenny. She's nice. We eat dinner together. They wash-up, she offers. I watch through the doorway. He dabs soap-suds on her nose. She retaliates with a full beard and moustache. He pulls her close and kisses her, the foamy beard shared out equally. The twinkling ring on her finger drives ice into my heart. He's hers now, not mine. But still, she is nice.

He marches up the drive. In another uniform. The last he'll wear. He salutes us as we open the door. His pale lips are pressed into a stiff line. He takes off the hat and smiles uncertainly. I want to cry. He's leaving us. Jenny holds my hand. She wants to cry too. He kisses us both goodbye. His mouth is not the soft baby pout of long ago.

He's coming home tomorrow. I insisted. Told them every journey he ever went on started here, at home. So this one must too. I refused Wootton Bassett, the folded flag, bugle and salvo. They agreed. They're sending a car. With a box. He won't smile when he sees us this time. He won't even know he's here. But he'll be home.

HOME TOMORROW
by Craig Irvine

Yesterday I was in the city. It's a different place to Middlesbrough. Strange street names, black iron fences and people, people, people. It's never dark; lights on every wall, every ceiling, in every window. But it's never really light. The sun hides behind tall buildings, even at its highest. In January it's never at its highest.

If you want to work, you've got to get out there. That's what my Mum says. So I was in the grey suit I hardly ever wear (too tight round the shoulders, too loose in the seat) threading my way between the natives of this place whose rhythm and beat I interrupt with my half-steps and shuffles.

About midday I found a bench. I was well ahead of schedule so I sat down and fumbled around in my backpack for the ham sarnie my Mum had wrapped in enough cling-film to stop a bullet. It was definitely one of those benches where a town planner had thought, "hmm, let's give people somewhere to sit but not let them get too comfortable."

So I'm sat there, wondering who GAV is who decided to tag my bench in neon green, and I'm wondering if GAV would know who the statue in the centre of the square is supposed to be. Heroes and villains of a foreign land.

While I'm sat there – fighting the Kevlar cling-film and noticing the ghosts of strangers that the people walking by will probably never notice in their lives – while I'm sat there, I start skipping songs on my sister's pink iPod. Mine ran out of charge before I came so I'm stuck with gangsta crap, not the chilled flow of slick hip-hop.

And while I'm flicking through tracks with one hand, this woman (hunched, hurrying and humourless) walks straight past me like I'm not even sat there and knocks the sandwich out of my hand. What the fuck?!

A couple of days ago I was leaving my parents' house. My Dad was putting up a fence out front. He held a hammer out to me, meaty fingers wrapped around its shaft.

"An Englishman's home is his castle," he said.

I took the hammer and joined in giving him his excuse to have a conversation. Yes, I was going for that interview. Yes, I was still listening to that black music. No, I hadn't seen my sister's iPod.

Left as soon as I could.

Today I'm sitting in the window seat watching Yorkshire spin by. Definitely gonna get one of those smartphones so I can always listen to DJ Shadow, De La Soul, Chali 2Na and 2Pac Shakur. Who wants to go live in the city anyway? Supposed to be a sunny day tomorrow so I might meet my girlfriend on the curvy benches in front of the library, maybe drift through the town centre. Keep it chilled.

Tomorrow.

HOME IS WHERE?
by Kieth Jackie

Trapped on a stinking bloody Stagecoach bus, you would have thought the driver would have had the sense to wake me. My name is Tom, I've been homeless now for five years and an alcoholic for four and eleven months. It's been a difficult month but I'm getting there. The thing is when you're a down and out, people are quite passive, so I tend to get left alone. The only trouble is, since I quit the drink last month I've developed some kind of narcoleptic sleep pattern. The doctor says I need to take it easy, but come on. How does an ex-alcoholic trying to drag his arse out of a bedsit and reintegrate himself into the world find time to take it easy? Although, truth be told, I've always been one for taking it easy, that's how I got myself into this mess of a life in the first place. Get an apprenticeship they used to say, get a good footing on the ladder, son, something to fall back onto. Well, what a load of bollocks that was; at sixteen I was well on the way to a prosperous career with the British Telecom.

I passed the entrance tests easy, but then things began to get difficult for me. The usual teenage dilemmas started to occur. I had parents who had suddenly woken up from their eternal bliss and realised the old marriage institution was a con, let the proceedings begin. The fights started so I packed up and left to stay with my older brother, that's when I found the entreating world of cigarettes and alcohol.

At the time, my brother was living with some other friends of his who had dropped out. While my bro was at uni I would be sat in the digs smoking weed and basically doing nothing. The fights started again with big bro – by now I was a bit older and street smart – so I thought I could handle the world. Within one year I was homeless and an incredibly talented junky. I say talented because not many junkies are known to have any talents, but I did. I would busk around the city centre and most days I would make a fair bob or two. I was drinking more and more. Life was fucking great.

That is until I caught sight of my own reflection. I met an old guy named Ivan, he was an artist and also a hopeless addict. I spent a few months with him and learnt a lot about the darkness of myself. I was a mess. The more shame I felt, the more smack I pumped into my veins – the more smack I was pumping, the more drink I needed to balance the books, if you know what I mean. Anyhow that was then, this is now, and right now I'm on my way to see my mother. Unfortunately, nobody bothered to wake the rough looking junky in the corner, so now I will have to wait till the morning before I can finally go home.

SIMPLY GIRLS
by Anita Kainthla

Every day, five near naked girls play outside my window. It's hard to guess their ages but they are roughly between 3 and 11 years. We all begin about the same time daily; me at my desk against the window, reading the newspapers, checking mail, and typing words on virtual paper and the five under-clad girls at their games I can't quite follow.

Saroj, the mother of the unclothed sisters, cooks and cleans for me. Saroj has six children; there is a son too. The five year old son is the father's favoured child whom he lugs around like an infant monkey. The rest of the brood is released at daybreak and herded up at dusk and in the in-between hours, they are as good as abandoned.

Saroj is young and attractive and taut, so that her saggy stretch-marked-stomach, drooping over the petticoat of her saree, seems like a misplaced identity.

She works with ferocious energy, doing incredulous amounts of work, in three households. She's perfected a method that keeps her employers fairly satisfied with her. If one day she skips brooming and mopping one house, the same day she advances an inability to cook at least one meal at another house. So each day manages to stretch her energy reserves to cover the operations of three households. If there's some grumbling by any of the employers, Saroj manages to wield it away with smooth talk. Other than that she barely talks.

There is a far away-ness in her demeanour which is hard to fathom. All she brings with her to work is her intent to get the day's work done. No idle chit chat, no personal questions. You can see the firm set of her jaw, the complete lack of acknowledgement of your query or instruction, the sudden grunts and sighs. She's dealing with the grime of her existence with every lash of the broom and every swish of the mop.

However, every few days she dispenses her angst without provocation:

"Only if that lout of a man would give me some of the money he earns. Only once a week he buys groceries. What do I put into the bellies of this long line of wretched children?"

"No money for kerosene; I should collect wood for cooking, he says. Some day I'm going to build a pyre and burn him on it."

And then nothing again for days, as though she's repenting for having indulged in such extreme expression.

The day we saw the last of her, she visited each one of us with her five daughters. Her last words were as few and potent as ever:

"That bastard has run away, madam. He's taken my son too. But that fool knows nothing. Only a woman can tell whose child she's carrying. He's taken off with another man's produce; serves him right for having denied his own flesh and blood, simply because they were girls.

I'm marrying my son's father; I will need a man."

DANIEL
by Lee Kelleher

I meet him in an American-style diner for lunch. He doesn't look particularly pleased to see me even though it has been over six months. His hair is shorter and graying. He looks around the restaurant. I remind him it's the closest place to his office and that I don't have much time.

"I don't have much time," he says.

My father lays out pictures of properties and their interiors with precision, all roughly the same distance apart. He matches them with small colour sample cards and moves them around repeatedly. The fan above my father's head spins around slowly, desperate to stop. I concentrate on this for a couple of minutes. I have nothing to think about, I realise. I almost smile but stop myself suddenly. I look at my father for a long time before he says anything. He takes small paper clips from his leather folder and attaches the colour cards to the appropriate photograph. He moves these to one side and takes out a magazine, its pages white and glossy. He turns the pages quickly, ripping out the articles he wants and placing them in front of me – the only free space on the table. There is a feature on health, a new restaurant, a club, a recipe and Las Vegas. He takes out some of the ads too. He doesn't look at me when he talks.

"How is the house?"

"I won't know until I get back."

"Tell me how it goes. I'm thinking about investing up there again." He makes eye contact.

We wait for the food.

"Would you like to work for me this summer?"

I look up at him.

"Renovations, mostly. You would be out of that workplace, in different properties every week. You would be stretching yourself. You would also meet people with serious... people who have a say."

After we have eaten I wait at the side of the restaurant and look out of the tall glass windows. My father pays the bill at the other side of the building. It is so bright outside, so hot, that for a moment everything is the same. Everything is white. Sweat forms on my forehead. I walk out further until the shade meets the sunlight and stop as though I have reached as far as I can go. I watch the cars and motorcycles glide across the slick black tarmac as though they were invented for this kind of weather, this kind of place.

I turn and walk back to the restaurant, glad to be away from the heat, if only for a minute. The restaurant is cool and my father is walking towards me. The table we sat at is in near darkness and my eyes struggle to make it out. The empty plates and glasses sit there waiting to be collected, surrounded by small sample cards of different colours – all evidence of a lunch enjoyed or a meeting gone well, perhaps. The fan above the table clicks and stops.

LUIGI AND THE MISADVENTURES OF A BROKEN TIME MACHINE
by Jim King

Once, there had been a man.

This man had been a man of science, of the depths of reasoning, and of religion, of exploring the very barrels of faith, and of mystique, and of mythology, and of stories passed down throughout the ages from father to son.

His name was Luigi (given upon rebirth).

And Luigi had fashioned a beautiful creature out of steel and iron and originality and daring and cunning and brilliance and madness and horror and wonder and fear.

You see, Luigi was born July 1960. He had been rather wretched up in an Italian life with the most uncaring of Italian families. No one had cared for the smallest. No one had cared too much for little Luigi, and so as a child, he had the idea that this…

…This crowning cesspit of ridicule and debauchery was not his home. A place void of love was not home. And he carried himself with tomorrow's thoughts.

"Perhaps I will find my new home tomorrow."

So forty-seven years on, and Luigi had fashioned a time machine. And only did he stop when he was no longer able to work. When his back was too far-out, and his bones ached, and his fingers bled, and by this time, it was more than ready.

But poor Luigi had handicapped himself from the very beginning.

And as he began, one day, to travel further back in time, he carried on forgetting about the miraculous tomorrow. With each journey, it flew further away.

"1860, then I'll go back," he told himself.

"1760, then I'll go back," he told himself.

"1660, then I swear, I'll go back," he forgot to cry aloud.

And by 1559, Luigi Dot was the most frustrated man in history. He pressed hard at every knob, and tugged at each cullet of wiring. And with no avail, he cried out to something that he had forgotten wasn't even there.

Luigi Dot remembered his name, and told the air, "I have done so much that it hurts. I just want home. Take me back. I implore you. Take me away."

And Luigi had now fallen so far back out of time that he was trapped in an immortal black hole.

And as he pondered ways of escaping a pointless routine-existence, he saw the dark, dark black hole grow eternal light. And from it, walked a sweet-smelling man, clothed in white robes.

"I have a command for you," said the Man. "Destroy this machine. Set it up in flames. And I will take you back."

"Can you take me home. Please, please do so, my good fellow. For I cannot take the pain of time any longer."

"I shall take you home."

"And yet, that would be impossible. For I know not where home is."

And the shining man turned and said something that neither I, nor Luigi Dot, and I hope nor you, would ever forget as long we were to live.

"Home is Tomorrow."

ALFIE AND THE HOME
OF TOMORROW
by Andrew Kirby

Alfie was holed up in the hotel room, trying to program the Teasmade so it didn't interfere with the picture on the widescreen TV. It was no good. He shook his head, returned to the bed and collapsed onto it, tucking his arms underneath his head. "Home Tomorrow," he thought. The end of the Ideal Home exhibition couldn't come quick enough for him. Nobody seemed interested in even pausing to look at his stand, let alone engaging him in conversation. Nobody thought they needed what he had to sell. It felt like rejection. Like a rejection of his dreams.

Alfie used to be obsessed with those sciencey TV programmes about 'The Home of Tomorrow'. He filled his scrapbook with pictures he cut out of the accompanying magazine series. TVs the size of walls, a pod in which to park the flying car where the TV aerial should have been. All straight lines and no fuss. And no Dad passed out on the heat-reflective carpet. He pasted in pictures of Sugar-Puff-faced robots too, helping out with the hoovering, serving Dad his home-from-work G and T as soon as he'd kicked off his work-shined shoes, giving Mam a hand with the washing up. He'd always wondered about that one. How could a robot go near water? Surely it messed with the wiring or something? Or maybe the robot just did the drying and putting away.

Later, when it was time for him to make his choices at school, he couldn't decide on architecture or science. Couldn't decide whether the best thing to help his family would have been improving the design of their living space or improving what actually went on within it. Giving Mam a bit of moral support while Dad pretended he was looking for a job and instead cluttered up the house with discarded racing pages and those little blue pens which could only have come from the bookies.

Later still, when the apocalyptic Years of Tomorrow, 1984, 1989, the millennium, 2012 had passed, and still not even the Japanese, renowned experts in the world of robotics, had managed to create a robot which could do anything other than launch weapons, Alfie started to regret his choice.

And even later, when he'd spent all his money on the stand at the exhibition in one last shot at proving that his own invention was the type of thing every home needed, and swiftly discovered that they didn't, all he could think was, "Home Tomorrow, and an end to this humiliation." Problem was, nobody thought they needed a robot to cure loneliness now. Not when they were so numbed by everything else going on in their homes, by their smart phones, their game stations, their dishwashers. Nobody needed a robot just to stand there with them while they polished the cutlery, looking out over the night sky at all those other tiny lights of civilisation.

"Home Tomorrow", and Sugar-Puff-faced Alf13 would be waiting, absolutely delighted to see him.

HOME TOMORROW
by Lynne Lawson

He always knew he would be home tomorrow, that tomorrow would be the day he finally made it back and all the pain would be forgotten. It was the thing that had kept him going on his darkest days and made the daily drudgery worth it. Just one more day, tomorrow he would be home.

This morning as his stiff, cold body woke to the sounds on the streets; the dustbin men, the office workers rushing by, coffees in hand, the occasional birdsong above the noise of the traffic, that same thought made him get up, gather his belongings and move on to roam the streets looking for a new place to sit.

Some days were good days; a warm doorway, a passer-by would smile and drop some change in his tin or on really good days they might buy him a sandwich or a coffee. Other days were dark; yesterday a lady dressed in expensive designer clothes looked down her nose at him and had actually kicked him as she went by. It could have been an accident but then, if it were, surely she would have apologised, acknowledged him, something, but no, she had hurried on by as if nothing had happened.

There she was again, designer shoes, handbag and the smell of the perfume, he knew that smell from happier days, his wife wore it. He shut out the thoughts; not today, he couldn't remember, it was too painful but tomorrow would be different.

He wondered if the people rushing by, busy with their own lives, even saw him, sitting on his blanket, bags by his side; not today, though it is cold and raining they have their heads down, big coats on. Two children nearby are jumping in puddles; they must be about 5 or 6, laughing, they don't care that it's cold, there's too much fun to be had splashing each other. How old are his own children now? 10, 11 maybe; he blocks the thoughts of them out, too painful, but tomorrow he'll see them again.

He knows if the weather is bad the queue for the hostel will be long; maybe he'd better make his way there now, and at least he will get some warm soup, maybe a wash and a real bed to sleep in. Things he used to take for granted but now every day is a struggle. He wonders if his family realise how lucky they are in their small cosy home. Did they think about him, wonder what he was doing? Well tomorrow he would tell them, tomorrow everything would be okay.

The hostel was full, he was too late; never mind, he knows a good doorway, sheltered and not too many people walk by to disturb him. He puts out his blankets; somehow they have stayed dry despite the rain. He sleeps.

The next day as his stiff, cold body wakes, he knows he will be home tomorrow.

NO. 6
by Callum Lister

I always found myself outside this door. Good days I would lean against the door frame with my forearm, a smile on my face that gleamed teeth. Knock, knock knock. Bad days I would sit on the kerb outside, hunched over my stomach.

There was nothing behind the door, there never was, until it was struck. The sequence, a light in the upstairs hallway, the sound of footsteps, the buckling of wood under foot, each step closer to reality, the light behind the door, finally the fumbling of locks. The open door revealed the kitchen.

Polar white and offensively lit, some days the buzz of the fluorescent tube would leave you with a headache. Some days the buzz of the wasp, bouncing from the window, would leave you with a headache. There was always a smell in the kitchen, always changing, always in flux. Some days it was like cat piss, underlying was the lonely smell of neglect.

It was this light perfume that crept around the door, chased by the weak hint of gas from the kitchen. It kept itself a secret. She kept herself a secret.

She unveiled her crooked teeth; they added character.

"Well, aren't you coming in?"

She always had that hurried tone to her. Busy, busy, busy. Some days it made me feel a little unworthy. Some days it made me feel expected. I usually stepped into the house. It was rare that I didn't, she had to come all the way down from the attic, I'd been waiting outside, routine was in motion. I walked straight upstairs, glimpsed myself in the mirror. It seemed like there was nothing but fire and ash behind me, every step left a trail of destruction behind me. Didn't look for too long, couldn't; I scared myself.

I carried on upstairs. The prints my feet left downstairs had begun eating away at the carpet, leaving charred prints. They spread across the floor, climbing the walls and curtains. I carried on up into the attic. The hallway light flickered off. I watched the back of her thighs. I could feel heat.

We kissed by her bed. Flames in the living room began to lick paint off the ceiling. Walls began to sweat. We made love. Fire ate away the lower floor of the house, fuelled by the sepia haze from the kitchen. Gas, that silent killer. It rushed up the stairs faster than she ever could. Fire would turn to ash, ash would turn to dust.

All that would remain was us, in that attic room, suspended in that infinite space. The smoke crept in following the heat. The door would burn with your coat on the back. We'd never notice this, not until the flames lashed you, pulled you away, wrapped you up, devoured you. Then there would be Destruction and I. In the infinite attic. Alone.

You always found me outside your door. Bad days you wouldn't answer, laid in apathy, trapped within yourself, waiting for a vibration in your pocket, a call to answer, a call to power, a call to being. Knock, knock knock. Good days you'd be waiting, the door framing you, a smile in your eyes and a kiss on your lips.

HOME TOMORROW
by Mark Lund

Davinia wasn't house-proud, she was house-scared. The faux-mansion in the North Yorkshire countryside seemed to goad her constantly; the shrill demands for attention heard from windows smeared with pigeon excrement; the mournful sigh of dust on sideboard; the threats and insinuations from muddy footprints on the hall carpet.

It had been so much easier when she had help appeasing the beast; she commanded an army of help who sponged, vacuumed, dusted, brushed and tickled every crevice until it gurgled with pleasure. This was before Martin had been expelled from the fourth boarding school.

Her husband's connections had managed to get Martin into Cranmore, the most expensive prep school in the country. Four previous expulsions meant that Martin's parents had been politely directed elsewhere by schools within their price range.

So the help had to go. Twelve rooms were effectively sealed off, casualties of a war Davinia knew she was losing. Ground was being ceded constantly as filth and decay issued ransom notes typed in Mother Nature's grimy font.

Her eyes dropped to the picture she was polishing; Martin at 4 years old, meeting the camera's gaze unsmilingly like a Victorian patrician. Not that Martin was a dour child – he would often cackle with glee at the most inappropriate moments.

The image of her son clapping and giggling at the fourth storey window from which his nanny had just hurtled to her death was one that still made her shudder; he was only 6 then and clearly didn't understand what had happened. When Davinia had placed her hand on his shoulder, he had stopped laughing and spun around to face her; for a fraction of a moment, an expression of fear widened his icy-blue eyes and drew his lips back from his unusually sharp teeth.

His face then returned to its naturally stern expression as he brushed past Davinia's leg, walked carefully around a spilled ashtray and left the room.

Accidental death had been the verdict. This didn't stop the whispers at the Women's Institute, the accident coming so soon after the previous nanny had taken her own life; Martin had silently directed his mother to the girl's room, dragging her insistently by the hand to witness the body hanging from a thin noose constructed from stockings and hair-dryer flex.

An overturned bottle of nail varnish had soaked its crimson contents into the carpet; Davinia would forever associate the bitter tang of its fragrance with the sight of the girl's gently swaying corpse.

She shook her head to dissolve the image, as if her memory was a kaleidoscope that could reassemble it into something less disturbing. Martin was home from school tomorrow and she would have to manage alone.

Her husband was in hospital; the motor oil on his boot leading to an incident on the kitchen floor that had earned him a fractured skull.

Martin was home tomorrow. He had better not make a bloody mess.

SETTING OFF TO ASIA
by Caitlin Macgregor

In an old, dusty countryside named Mere Town lived three children with their Grandma. The oldest child was called Corey who was twelve, and the second child was called Toby, he was nine and the third was called Caitlin, she was three years old. The children were doing fine but Gran wasn't – she had been laying down for weeks now.

Corey and Toby walked to a place far away to get some water. That's exactly why their Mam walked all the way to Asia to family. There were too many riots and fights and stuff like that.

Grandma was starting to feel better so they knew it wouldn't be long for Gran to be okay again. It was now time for Corey and Toby to go back to school. They managed to get the right amount of money to pay for school. Toby moaned after half an hour of walking but they were only half way there. Corey was used to walking so far. Six hours later lessons had finished.

"You can go home now children, goodbye," said the teacher, so Corey and Toby walked out of the classroom as quick and as bright as a firework. When they got home, Caitlin was still in the same place she was when Corey and Toby left for school. She was in the same position and Gran commented on that and if Gran commented on it, then it was no joke. Gran and Corey had a talk about Caitlin. Toby heard and got really upset; his heart sank like a ship sinking under water very quickly. He darted to his bedroom. Corey knew he had heard and chased him to his bedroom to see if he was okay. Corey and Toby talked about Caitlin and Corey told him it's not a worrying point because they don't know if she was just tired. But not long after, Caitlin was poorly; she was getting very hot. Grandma ordered Caitlin to bed because they were stressing her out.

Next morning Caitlin rushed into Grandma's room, "Grandma, why don't we go to Asia?"

"No way," said Grandma, "go back to bed, it's four o'clock in the morning."

She was as tired as ever and she crawled back into bed.

Three hours later Corey woke up and went to see Caitlin. She was much worse. She was vomiting and now Toby had come to see. Toby started to cry and it was hard for Corey to calm him down. Finally Corey managed to calm Toby down so they went and got dressed for school. Today was a big test so they couldn't miss school but Corey didn't care, neither did Toby, so they set off half an hour late.

On their way, a women ran towards them as if she knew them. As they got closer they realised it was their Mam. Corey rushed over to tell her about Caitlin. She rushed home with some medical money. Grandma was so happy to see her. They got ready and dashed to get some medical help. Luckily a lady helped out nearby.

SOLEMNITIES AND CIGARETTES
by Liam Macleod

I hate having to wear me smart gear. The jacket's me Dad's so it's effing massive, making the shirt and trousers look even smaller. That's probably the worst thing about smart clothes, they're so thin and tight it's like they're constantly threatening to split. I want to be back in jeans and a t-shirt, outside Harrington block, smoking a rollie, instead of the Tesco car park with a box of Lambert and Butler. It doesn't help my mood then when Beth walks up wearing Matty's red hoody over her smart blouse and a skirt so long a nun'd find it chaste.

"Thought I'd find you here," she says, sitting down next to me.

"Well, you're about the only one that did, even Dad didn't spot me when he stopped off for milk."

"So when did you start smoking?"

"Few weeks after I left, just joints at first but when the weed ran out, guess it stuck."

"Let us 'ave one then." I chuck her the pack but she can't light it one-handed with all the wind, so I have to lean in and block out the cold.

"Not really my type these, I'm usually a Superkings lass, or I was anyway."

"Aye, I usually roll my own but I can't do it out here 'cos of the wind and they kicked me out of Costa Coffee when I tried to roll in there."

"Do you wanna go for a pint in the Cons Club, they'll probably let you roll."

"You sound just like Matty. Every time we went out it had to be the Cons, he wouldn't go anywhere else."

"Even more reason we should go, our own little tribute to him."

"Haven't we done enough of that today?" When I turn, Beth is already looking to the floor. "I'm sorry, I didn't mean that."

"Then why'd you say it? What the fuck's the matter with you, why're you even out here?"

"I know, I know, it's retarded, I just couldn't go home, not yet."

"Why, what's so bad at home?"

"Nothing just, well that's it, nothing. If I'd gone home Dad would've put the telly on, Mum'd make the tea and it would've been over. People up here don't grieve, they survive. They watch telly, they go out to Tesco for milk. They don't sit around car parks sulking. To them death's just a day off work." Beth looks at me, shocked.

"How can you even say that? You think we don't grieve, you think today was just a day off work for me?" When she breaks down I hold her, feeling like the world's biggest shit as she sobs. After a while I offer to go to the Cons Club, it's dingy and full of old men but I can roll there. She orders a vodka and coke and I get a bottle of Newcastle Brown and we make our tribute quietly. Tomorrow I can get the train back to London, back to my life.

HOME TOMORROW
by Michael James McAllister

Tommy Kelloe of the Parachute Regiment had phoned his wife the previous evening and told her that he would be home tomorrow. He flew into Brize Norton from Afghanistan the next day at two in the afternoon and hitched a lift into Oxford. Facing a long wait for his train he decided to go for a pint to kill the time.

Fruitless attempts to get served at three pubs and running the gauntlet of abusive comments because he proudly wore the full uniform of the Parachute Regiment had surprised and angered him. Disconsolately Tommy made his way back to the station.

Several lengthy delays caused by a light coating of snow meant that by the time he got to his hometown station, Tommy had missed the last bus and set off to walk the mile or so home. He was almost within sight of his house when he saw a gang of three youths pelting bricks at a security guard on a building site. He confronted the three hooligans and told them to go home.

The biggest of the three, a tall gangly youth, pulled a kitchen knife from his belt and Tommy used his haversack to fend off several attempts to stab him. One of his mates had sneaked behind Tommy and hit him over the head with a lump of wood while the third gang member, a rat faced youth, had also pulled out a knife and stabbed him in the legs.

His head throbbed and his vision was blurred and blood oozed through his trouser legs. He went for the lad with the lump of wood and he backed away. Meanwhile the big lad and rat boy attacked, stabbing him in the back and chest as he turned to confront them. He was weakening quickly from blood loss and slumped against the fence.

The thugs rifled his pockets and took the haversack with the presents for his wife and baby. They had been through all of his pockets except one. A small blood soaked photo was plucked from Tommy's breast pocket by the taller of the thugs. He could smell the cider and glue on their breaths and helplessly watched as the callous thug tore into pieces the photo of his newborn son.

Tommy could barely move and with his lifeblood ebbing away reached for the fragments of his photo close to his feet. With a great effort of will he managed to scoop two pieces into his hand.

Under a dim street light he tried to focus his fading sight, but all he could see was a blood-stained baby's head in a small fragment and the lower half of his wife's body in a larger piece.

He recalled a few lines from his favourite poem. "O it's Tommy this and Tommy that, an' Tommy go away. But it's thank you, Mr Atkins, when the band begins to play." Tommy's band played its last note in a building site half a mile from home.

HOME TOMORROW
by Fiona McLanders

The wind stings my face as I push the stubborn old gate shut. Stiff, more rotten than ever, its corroded hinges squeal like a dying rodent. The gardens look as bleak now as when I first arrived after our holiday romance, became the famer's wife, eighteen, head full of dreams.

Sheltered by the wall lie rows of beds where Joe's onions, potatoes and cabbages grew, behind it the decaying greenhouse, where his mother used to grow her precious tomatoes.

Not a flower in sight, there never was.

"Can't eat a flower," Joe's mother said, "so what's the point? Everything must earn its keep."

But flowers were my ticket home. The scent of jasmine at the garden centre near here, or bread at the village bakery, could whisk me back. For a glorious fleeting moment, I'd be on our whitewashed terrace overlooking the sea, my mother's loaves baking in the oven with a rosemary-studded leg of lamb, the smell of warmth, well being.

For the last time, I take the shale path to thorny higher ground, where sheep grazed until two weeks ago. It's silent now, apart from the wind whipping the sycamores into submission. The smell of stale turnips stains the air. For nearly twenty years, always the same routine. The daily drudgery of herding the beasts up to higher pasture and luring them down at night, whatever the weather.

I'm flanked by tumbling stone walls that slash through a hillside that's scarred with burned heather, ploughing up into crags, where the wind has polished every trace of grass off a sheer face that plummets into a lake so deep, it murmurs when the North wind blows.

The slumping roof of the cow barn is saddle backed by neglect. Where tiles are missing, the timber frame protrudes like the ribcage of a fallen dinosaur and a sapling oak tree pokes out. Inside the wooden sheds, tractor parts lie festering in the rutted dirt.

Shadows dapple the fields, dark clouds scud across a slate sky. Joe's tools, a scythe, two spades and a rake, lie abandoned in the grass. I cross the yard, swatting the sticky black flies that infiltrate the house in summertime, settling on every surface, rash-like.

Inside, stripped of its furnishings, naked and forlorn, the house resounds with the echoes of a hollow life lived in a straightjacket of boredom.

"Isabella, time to go," Victoria calls. "Don't want to miss the plane." I smile at her, my pretty younger sister, my rock since Joe's funeral.

I feel a drop on my cheek, "There's the rain."

"Who cares? It's hot today, in Spain," she says smiling, as I slip the car out of the driveway. "We'll be home tomorrow in time for a dip in the pool, perhaps drinks to toast your new apartment, before dinner at Luigi's with Mama and Papa?"

Driving down the lane, in twenty years that's the best view I've had of this place. It looks great in my rear view mirror.

SIX YEARS
by Matthew Miller

Jack had been dissatisfied, though the exact source of this dissatisfaction, or for how long it had been building up, he was unable to place. His motives had been muddied by endless self-assessment.

Married, with children, two girls, a good steady job, sales manager, healthy salary. He took care to leave little trace of himself. Cash-in-hand jobs, no car, no bank account, off the radar.

He was going home tomorrow. Even the decision had lifted a weight. He had always convinced himself that it was too late to turn back. Today, he had made his first positive decision since leaving.

He didn't sleep well that night, the same confused thoughts and dreams stealing into his skull uninvited, bouncing around, creasing his brow, finally dissipating, replaced by yet more disturbing images. He watched himself return and drive his car through the front of the house into the living-room. He stepped out, grinning, set fire to the carpet, watched his family passively through a wall of flames. He stared through the window as his youngest daughter opened the garden gate and ran away. She wasn't coming back and he smiled contentedly.

He woke the next morning, head groggy, and sat for an age on the edge of the narrow mattress, running his fingers through his hair, massaging his scalp, trying to coax calm from his thoughts. He filled the sink in the corner of the room, washed himself, selected clothes from the suitcase by the bed.

The journey took several hours, in a car bought for the occasion. As he approached the house, he was overcome by a wave of sickening nostalgia. He had come back this way before, never intending to make contact, and each time had sat in a trance, letting the last six years wash over him, basking in his own cowardice.

Not this time.

He stepped from the car, shoes resounding on the pavement, the ground quaking with each uncertain step. Six years of suppressed emotion welling, ready to burst. He felt so happy as his knuckles met solid oak, once, twice, three times. He heard footsteps and imagined holding his daughters high, pressing his wife to him and promising never to let them go.

He was so ready.

The door opened. Jack stepped back, breathing hard, head flipping, hands shaking.

"Can I help you?"

She seemed genuinely concerned, though it was all Jack could do not to scream at the banality of the question.

"Where's Sarah?"

The reduction of the momentous situation to the utterly mundane twisted his gut.

"I'm afraid she hasn't lived here for some time. She left her contact details, I'm sure I can find them...."

But Jack was already back in his car and driving away. It was too late. He would find a Bed 'n' Breakfast tonight and be back home tomorrow. Home.

He could have taken the details of course. He could have followed them. But he knew he wouldn't have made the call.

Not for another six years.

POSITIVE THINKING
by Kath Morgan

I say the words over and over, thinking if I just keep on saying them, they'll come true. Positive thinking, that's what my Mum calls it. Lots of her friends have started doing it. No kidding. Ever since my mum conjured up Alfie. She says she found him through the power of positive thought. All her mates think she's brilliant, some kind of guru or something. But they don't know Alfie, do they?

There were these little rituals she'd go through. She'd wait 'til I was in bed but I'd always know when to listen in 'cos she'd light a candle and the stink of ylang ylang would drift up and make me want to sneeze. I wouldn't though, 'cos she'd have heard me and stopped.

My eyes search the space around me. Light spills in through a high narrow window that runs along one wall, but there's no sign of any candles. I'll just have to do without. I can still do the voice.

Let him be tall, she'd say.

Let him have a good job.

Let him be kind.

Let him have a sense of bloody humour.

Nothing like my Dad then.

She'd say each bit three times for luck, in a soft slow rhythm like my teacher's voice would go whenever she read poetry to us, which she liked to do a lot. I can't believe I used to complain about that. I'd give anything to hear Wordsworth again.

I take a deep breath.

"I'll be home tomorrow."

Long pause.

"I'll be home tomorrow."

Pause.

"I'll be home tomorrow."

I must have fallen asleep then, 'cos the next thing I know someone is pulling my arm, yanking me to my feet, saying, "A looker, Alfie said. Come on, then, let's get a look at you."

I blink sleep from my eyes, and hunger hits me at the same time as the fact that there's three of them, all staring, all hairy, all stinking of the same smell as Alfie's got. Like sweat, only sharper. Something... hormonal.

"He'll do," the man in the middle says, his eyes scanning me like he's at a checkout. I press my back into cold brick as he leans forwards and takes hold of my elbow, but there's nothing I can do. My hands are tied tight behind me, and anyway, I'm too weak from hunger to fight.

"I'll be home tomorrow," I whisper fiercely as he leads me across an enclosed yard to the open boot of his car. He wraps a gag around my mouth and pushes me into the dark. My cheek rests on cold metal that stinks of oil. The engine roars its vibrations into my empty belly. Snot and tears dry on my face as I drift in and out of sleep.

Then BAM.

Tyres screech.

Silence.

Loud voices.

Sirens. Lots of sirens.

I kick my legs and squeal through the gag.

Bright light.

Helmets.

A voice.

"It's okay, son. You're alright now. You're going home."

HOME TOMORROW
by Jaime Moussa

"**B**ut you're going to die!"

Her voice was taut, her eyes burned.

"Well, it's good to know you can just write me off," I snapped. I sounded angry. I had meant to sound deeply hurt. The Steadicam looked up at us in pieces from the floor, waiting patiently to be assembled. My daughter trembled in her anger, like a small metal teapot on the hob. I tried again.

"Look, I understand these things. I'll help you. We'll make it together."

I could tell she didn't want to do this with me. Why did the young always want to take over? Had I been like this at 25? If so, I repent.

"What am I going to do when you're not here to help?" There she goes again. Killing me off.

Her eyes brim up.

"Don't get upset, darling. Come on. Let's not fight."

I still feel 18. An 18 year old in this tent of a 70 year old. The last 10 years has been full of younger men, trying to get rid of me. Time is up, they say. I never thought my own daughter would feel that way.

She looks forlornly at the nuts and bolts at her feet. She thinks this is the end. Young people are so dramatic. They think the smallest obstacle is life ending. She doesn't realise she's just beginning.

"You're talented, you know. You'd work this out if you had to."

This world, this age of new things, is home for her. And it starts tomorrow. Tomorrow is familiar to her. For me, it was yesterday. I just want her to tell me that I can still succeed at some things.

My eyes burned, my voice was angry, but inside I was like a cornered rodent. Frightened. I glanced at him. He was hurt. He thought

I was calling him old. Can't he see? It wasn't because I couldn't put together a Steadicam on my own. It wasn't about the stupid Steadicam at all. The Steadicam had simply awakened the fear. That piece of equipment represented my life, in bits, on the floor. And one day, my daddy wouldn't be there to help me put it together.

"Who's going to help me? I might not get married, you know." I probably never will. Too much hurt. I'll have to build this horrible machine alone. Without my Daddy.

He gets to go to his maker. His struggle through the crowds of life are soon over. Lucky him. He gets to go home. Knowing he did a great job. I get left in a world so foreign. A world – Daddyless.

"Sorry, Daddy."

I just want him to tell me that one day I will succeed without him.

A PLACE CALLED HOME
by Rebecca Muddiman

Three years is a long time. Long enough for a place to become home anyway. The place I call home is a seven-by-seven cell I share with Bill the Bollock. This little square box with peeling walls and piss-streaked floors. This is my home, my little sanctuary in a concrete slab show-home for scumbags.

Outside these four walls, where the animals roam, isn't for me. Out there is kind of like what other people, normal people, must experience at work, I reckon. You have to be on your guard all the time. People looking over your shoulder with every move you make. Arseholes telling you what you can and can't do. Yeah, there'll be couple of lads you think are alright and in another life you might actually go to the match with one of them. But most of them are total knobs. You don't tell them that though, you just nod at them as you pass and hope they don't start talking to you 'cause you know that if that happens you'll never escape. In the real world it's boring conversations and bad breath that'll do you in. In here it's funny looks and affiliations. And probably homemade weapons as well. So I keep my head down. The best thing to do is just be nothing. Be nobody. Just exist. That's what Bollock told me my first night.

Just exist.

I kind of expected trouble from a guy called Bollock but he's alright really. Full of wisdom, so he thinks. Says he's never getting out. I don't think he wants to - he seems to like it. But he's glad I'm getting out. "Home tomorrow," he keeps telling me as I peel my picture of some Page 3 bird off the wall. He grins every time he says it and I nod back at him but I don't say a word. Thing is, I want to get out, 'course I do. Who'd want to stay? Except Bollock, that is. The only problem with 'Home Tomorrow' is I don't know where home is anymore. Kelly won't take me back. I doubt she's even at the flat anymore. She's probably moved in with some bloke who doesn't turn over when America's Next Top Model is on. Our Mam won't have me back and who can blame her? She doesn't deserve it. She's had enough.

I guess they'll find me something. Maybe a little room with peeling walls and piss-stained floors. Some little place I can call home.

Yeah, that'll do me.

HOME TOMORROW
by Will Nett

This story doesn't pretend to be something it's not; it knows it's a five hundred word piece based on the theme of 'Home Tomorrow'. It knows about the £500 prize money too, and that there's already around forty quid's-worth here. 'Home Tomorrow'. I keep leaning towards the sci-fi element that those words seem to invoke to me but probably everyone else does too: tales of lost astronauts returning to earth, or their equivalent planet, to find that they were better off where they were, that kind of thing.

Otherwise, I could simply fabricate an encounter between Sherlock Holmes and the little-known arch villain, Dr Tomorrow, or boxer Larry Holmes' low-profile tussle with African heavyweight, Obafemi Tomorrow. I'm writing this at home on the day the competition was launched and wondering whether to submit it straight away or wait until nearer the closing date so it doesn't get submerged under the deluge of car chases and unrequited love stories set on train station platforms. I could send it off the day after today, which is Wednesday, and according to the Oxford English Dictionary, tomorrow, but I suppose it depends when you read it that determines when I wrote it.

According to Bryan Ferry, 'This is tomorrow...' If he's right then today's a Tuesday. The Beatles thought that 'Tomorrow Never Knows'. Never knows what, though? What day it is? Probably. They were right about everything else though, and who am I to argue with a band that practically invented popular culture?

They also told us that 'She's Leaving Home', wherever that is. Whoever 'She' was, I wonder if she passed Dr Feelgood on her travels. They were 'Goin' Back Home', or so they said, as were John Denver, Simon and Garfunkel.

The word tomorrow doesn't appear in the Bible, however the

word home is used regularly. (You will now go and check this for yourself.)

"Home is where you live," somebody told me. That wasn't quite right. I've lived all over the place but I've only lived at home once.

Alexander Chase said that a man's home was his wife's castle. I say, who would dare argue? I bet Chase himself didn't.

There's two loud-mouthed Americans – is there any other kind? – presenting some baseball coverage on television as I write this. They're talking about home-runs and how they're both looking forward to tomorrow's big game.

The 5-string banjo songbook beside me is open at the page of Mitchell Jayne's 'Old Home Place'.

Ninety-one pounds of writing to go then. That's less than a century of words to say something of interest on the aforementioned subject. Maybe I've already done that, who knows? Tomorrow doesn't.

Just before I heard about this competition I was on the phone to my friend, Derek. He never says goodbye, he just hangs up after his last sentence. On this occasion, his parting line was, 'My pigeons should be home tomorrow.'

That was weird.

I submitted this the day before judging. Have I won? I'll let you know tomorrow.

HOME TONIGHT
by Paul O'Neill

I was shaving in the bath when I first heard her scream. So loud that I nicked myself. I didn't get out straight away. I just kind of lifted myself up onto my elbows in case she screamed again. Then she screamed again.

When I got downstairs she was by the door. She looked frightened but there was nobody else in the room. There was just the noise from the television in the corner. She looked pale.

"It was this big," she said with her hand out in front of her. "I was watching Gok and I saw it out of the corner of my eye."

I looked down at the blank space of carpet but I couldn't see anything. I wasn't sure what to say.

"It ran straight past the rug," she said, this time with the quiver that means tears. "Anyway," she said, "I'm not spending another night here until you've found it."

After she'd gone, I let my eyes roam around the furniture in the room: the television, the bookcase and the places things can hide. After a while I picked up the rug and shook it hoping that something would fall out. Nothing. I carried the lamp and the coffee table out of the room and set them down in the hallway. Next, I shoved the drinks cabinet across the floor whilst the bottles chinked against each other inside. With everything moved I sat on the carpet and thought about how different the room looked. I wondered if she'd seen anything in the first place. The phone rang.

"Hello," I said.

"Have you found it yet," she said.

"Where are you?" I said. "It sounds noisy."

"I'm having my nails done," she said, "and my hair. I needed to calm down. Have you found anything yet?"

I scratched my head. "No," I said. "Not yet." Then there were a few seconds of silence. I suppose we had both made clear what we wanted to say. I could hear the sound of women laughing in the background.

"Don't just pretend you've found it when I get home," she said, "because I'll know. I want to see it dead for myself. I won't be happy until I've seen it dead with my own two eyes." I was a little surprised by the way she put this.

"You do care about me, don't you, honey?" she said.

"Of course I do," I said, "I've spent the past two hours…"

"And you do want to make me happy don't you?" she said

"Trisha," I said, "you know I do."

"I know you do, sweetie. I might not be home tonight," she said. She made a loud kissing sound over the phone.

Then she was gone again. There was a strange echo around the room when I put the receiver down. In the street outside there was the sound of an ice-cream van and children shouting. Through the walls I could hear the sound of the neighbours arguing.

JUMPING THE QUEUE
by Bernie Petegou

"That's the house," Bryan says, pointing at it. "Lovely, isn't it?"

"It looks brilliant!"

Her face is glowing. Bryan expected it. The other punters had the same reaction. A three bedroom semi-detached house with driveway and front and back gardens is a dream for anyone desperate for a council house.

A couple of passers-by have got within earshot. Bryan waits for them to move on, and reminds himself that he needs to find a new bait house in a different part of town.

"Like I said on the phone, this could be your home tomorrow. You want to have a look?"

"Wow! How much is the rent?"

Bryan smiles to himself. She is well baked, but he must remain professional. This job requires more skills than armed robbery.

"Sixty-five to seventy a week," he says, leading her into the turfed front yard, expecting to hear something about a bargain.

"I pay a hundred and twenty where I live now, and it's not half as good!"

"Some landlords are proper conmen, aren't they? We can't go inside the house, because it's not empty yet, by law. But let's go round the side, so you can check the back garden."

"Fantastic! I can see the kids kicking a ball here. What do I need to do? It's not something illegal, is it?"

"Well, you've been bidding for houses now for what, two, three years? I can arrange for you to move in here tomorrow."

They walk through a high gate at the back of the house. It's quiet. The grass is overgrown, but the garden shed has had a fresh coat of redwood paint.

"I'm definitely interested," she says.

Bryan, calm as a solicitor, produces forms from Erimus Housing.

"This is what will happen. You sign here to say you're bidding for this house, and give me a hundred pounds. I go back to the office now, make this house officially vacant and put you down straight away as first bidder. The office will contact you in the morning as a priority, and they'll send a lady down to meet you with the keys, so you can have a proper viewing before signing the tenancy. But don't tell anyone about the money; I'll get sacked and they'll give the house to someone else. Are you happy with that?"

"Sure! I'll save a fortune on rent alone." She goes through her handbag, digs five Twenties out and hands them over. 'I thought you might ask for more than a hundred, to be honest."

"Naah! You scratch my back, I scratch yours."

She signs the forms.

"Keep checking the website, if they don't ring you first thing in the morning. Sometimes the system takes a while to update. You've got my mobile, haven't you?"

"Yes, I have, Bryan."

Bryan looks at her as if he has been hit by a potato harvester.

"Your real name's Bryan, isn't it?" she asks.

The two passers-by appear from nowhere and quickly restrain him.

"Police! You're under arrest, Bryan!"

NAB
by Claire Picken

"**B**ut flags are points," said Nab. "Why have I got only one for this?" The goblin stood, shuffling from one foot to the other.

"It's red, and only worth one point," said Torri the ogre, the leader of the summer camp for young goblins. "So far, that's all you've collected."

Nab grimaced and kicked at the hard ground. He had been certain these were blue, and worth a whopping six points.

"Looks like Spat's going to win the trophy this year. Forty-two points to his name so far." Torri stuck the score sheet under his nose and he nodded miserably. "Ten years in a row your family has had that trophy. All your brothers and sisters were champions. Now you're ten-years-old it's your turn. Your Dad will be disappointed if you go home tomorrow without it. Only chance you've got is to find that flag. You don't want to let your family down?"

Nab shook his head. "Thanks for the advice." He wondered how he'd know it even if he did find it, when he could only see black and grey. Being colour-blind had its drawbacks, but he preferred to keep it a secret, even from his best friends.

"Off you go," said Torri.

"Hey!" Spat jeered as he came out of the games tent. "That golden trophy is mine. Best accept you're a loser now…"

"You're not the winner yet!" cried Nab, marching away.

The only place no one had searched was around the hill known as Elf's Eyebrow, but everyone knew goblin-munching humans lived there with their slobbering pets. He'd have to be very careful…

"If I get caught and chucked into a stew they'll all be sorry," he mumbled and set off.

Not far from the camp a small mountain of rubbish had been dumped. The smell wafting from it was so delicious he couldn't resist stopping to see if anything tasty had been thrown away. Scrabbling about amongst some rotten pig snouts, he pulled a grey flag from the pile.

"How many points for this?" he thought stuffing it into his pouch. "I bet it's another red flag," he mumbled, biting his lip.

Outside the games tent, Spat was bragging the trophy would soon be his. "Found another red one?" he sneered.

Nab ignored him and went inside to join a small queue.

"What have you got now?" Torri said when it was his turn to show what he'd found.

"This," said Nab pulling the flag from his pouch.

"Well, well," Torri grinned, "thought we'd hid it so well none of you crazy bunch would find it. The golden flag earns you fifty points. Looks like you've won! Done your family proud!" she beamed.

"I... found... it?" stuttered Nab. His smile grew so big it almost split his face in two. He'd beaten Spat and he could go home tomorrow holding the golden trophy and make his family proud!

"Anything is possible, as long as you try hard enough." Spat grinned.

FOLLOW YOUR NOSE
by Dani Redd

A week before I left India, I pinned a small square of fabric I'd found to the side of my trousers. I hoped that it would absorb all the country's smells, and I'd be able to keep it as a memento when I returned home. I had presents of coloured fabric, of essential oils, and cheap fags, but for me the most important thing to take back from a country is the memory of its smell. It's the first thing that comes to you when you get off the plane, and take your first breath of un-recycled air; all countries smell different. The smells of India sometimes assaulted your nostrils like a slap in the face, making you reel, and other times they were infinitely more subtle. A man on the train from Madurai to Villapuram told me that India was characterised by an "overmuchness", and this was certainly true of the miasma of scent that hung over the country, as well as the excessiveness of its large population and oven-like heat. India smelled of fragrant bidi fumes, curls of incense smoke and the red mosquito coils, ripe fruit, rotting fruit. It smelled of car fumes, of the acrid red dust that blew everywhere, of sun-heat on gravel and on dirt, of the endless plastic rubbish being burnt. Of meat fry, hot oil, nuts being dry roasted in cast iron pans. Undeniably, the cities smelled patchily of urine and shit and the black slime-like detritus of the sewers. But there were lighter, whiter notes in this olfactory symphony: jasmine flowers, religious garlands, hot starry velvet nights, cool blue of the mountain air, pale sea breezes.

As my leaving date drew inexorably closer, I worried I would forget how India smelled, and that its colour would fade and the potency of each moment would be lost. But on the last day the inevitable shift occurred. I stopped worrying about forgetting, and started trying to remember what England smelled like. I knew, having lived and travelled abroad for long periods of time before, that I'd spend the first few days feeling like a stranger in my own country, isolated from the comfort offered by familiar rituals. Fish and chips would be exotic. I would spend far too long trying to count out change in the newsagents because the monetary values of the coins would no longer be ingrained in my consciousness. Maybe if I tried to remember what England smelled like it would feel more like home. I closed my eyes and remembered bonfire smoke, barbecue smells of charred meat, the smell of rain, compost, the local mud with its characteristic brick red colour. The thick, seaweed salt smell of the estuary near my home. Sweetness of cut grass in summer, of silage and farms. The gluey fumes from the cellophane factory near Bridgwater that float through the car windows driving down the M5. The smell of old booze and fags of the local pub, because even though there's been a smoking ban in place for a while, people having been smoking and drinking there for so long the walls are saturated in the scent. Or maybe it's just the memory of a scent that's gone, and just the idea of it remains. I find it hard to untangle them sometimes, smell and memory. Something tangible... and a ghost, a dream. But unfolding the fabric square, in the privacy and pale blue of my own bedroom, I crushed it to my nose and all I smelled was dirt. Somewhere along my journey home the melody of all those smells had been lost, or maybe they had never fixed themselves to the cloth at all. But, closing my eyes and breathing in, I felt as if I still remembered it, almost as well.

HOME TOMORROW
by Daniel Regan

"London." Never had the word been uttered so softly, precariously and exclusive of enthusiasm. Her weak smile attempted to belie internal trauma, a guise of an exceptionally contrived performance. The girl with the Chanel sunglasses no longer appeared the picture of serenity – I could sense she was uncomfortable. The anguish flooded across her face, her lips contorted and introverted, sinking into her mouth and teeth pressed awkwardly against lipstick. A frenetic, desperate glance to the right and her hair reluctantly followed. Motion rapidly decelerated and now only this single moment existed. The rest of the time, the assorted humans that made up the surrounding crowd were frozen into irrelevance.

Now the Chanel sunglasses were gone, plastic on the concourse, and there was nothing to insulate me from her piercing gaze. She was calling out to anyone, screaming for their help; her mouth didn't move but her eyes articulated desperation. Time resumed and her male encroachment was unimpressed. The sunglasses cracked against the concrete under his worn-down loafers. His fumbling, damp fingers found her bag and caressed the patent leather for valuation, barely able to conceal an inner pleasure. Within seconds he was gone with his new accessory, running across the concourse, ploughing through the crowd, ready to vault the ticket barriers. The girl, I think, was weeping.

I had watched the two characters intermittently from the café, and all I could do was smile. I was invigorated and repulsed by the perverse pleasure I was deriving from this girl's pain. I felt an adrenaline rush over my body, a symphonic melody that circumvented sensory perception playing from within, quite literally coming from the heart. I closed my eyes and my spatial consciousness slipped away. I was no longer anchored to the physicalities of the station.

I was content.

Four minutes later I decamped to platform 11. I briefly considered the unhealthy irony of subservience to sadistic feelings, but I was too tired to truly care. I surveyed the gathering mass with envy and intolerance; my fellow passengers were nauseating to behold. Irreverent teenagers plugged mindlessly into their iPods, with faces that epitomised and induced unadulterated boredom. Their voices coated with a sickening sheath of Sloane Ranger, pasted onto barely traceable, frustrated regional accents. They were intermingled between preposterously dressed businessmen and their smartphones, inseparable and conflated. I looked ahead to the window panels arbitrarily punched into the station wall. I focused onto the patches of simmering light that reflected from the glass, beige swathes of colour that began to coalesce and expose my Burberry trenchcoat.

Then there was me; a sickly, pathetic, disingenuous excuse for a face that barely hid a smug, pulsing misanthropy. The overhead power lines rippled and clicked under stress. The 19:00 to King's Cross banked a corner and twisted into view. I watched, as if by proxy or through bodily detachment, my mouth grimace and without stimulus grow into a smile. I was smiling. I knew that in five hours I would be home.

JIM AND MARILYN UPON THE DARKEST HIGHWAY
by James Robinson

Marilyn woke softly and peered out from the fraying blanket spread out across the passenger seat.

They were still moving.

She was curious as to how Jim had stayed awake all this time, and perhaps didn't want to know. Without so much as a twinge. For the car was in its usual state of competence, and there were no police for miles it seemed.

It was still so alike a dream. She was wrapped in warmth, and the daring lover was sitting right next to her, smiling like they did in the movies.

The dark circles were rushing along the road so fast, and the cold air hit the window once or twice. And to their left went the World, and with it, each scrap of metal trickling gas. And to the right, untouched forest. And ahead, only tomorrow.

"Who knows Jimmy, that right there in the dark might be our new home," Marilyn was hoping with each tendril of her heart.

"I really hope so, darlin'," Jim couldn't help but agree as he kept a gaze swivelling between the perils of the open highway and the adoration in her eyes.

And together, they couldn't have hoped any stronger, or wished any tighter.

After all, everyone deserved a home they gathered, and certainly it was their desire to believe that everyone deserved a tomorrow.

It was an accident.

There had been the police chase in New Jersey, after the first murder. But that wasn't meant to happen. Hardly had his finger slipped away that a single bullet came flying out into the man's chest. And it wasn't like he hadn't deserved it. He'd been raking for more than his fair share.

And hardly did the robbery in Atlanta seem a misdirection of justice. Desperation had kicked in days ahead, and they had come to the silent state for food, and shelter, and compassion. But none who once held their hands out would do so this time around, and so things (naturally) turned ugly.

But it was an accident.

And the bump. The one hiccup as the car jilted a tad. This was it, right now, the moment in which home and tomorrow or a twisted spectrum of the two was to intervene.

A single star rose in the night sky, like a burning glory among darker pathways. Marilyn slumped back in her chair, covered in the fraying blanket. What a dreadful existence this had attempted to become. Two star-crossed lovers as they knew one another, abandoned by God as they saw one another.

Jim stiffened, and rubbed his eyes. It was the star leading them home. A new home. And fragile as it seemed, they were not afraid of life anymore. Sirens had vanished long ago. There was a light; small but oh so alive. And there was something coming. Something special. And it called itself anew. A new tomorrow.

HOME TOMORROW
by Debbie Rosen

Thursday afternoon in the office. The clock moves towards five as I lurk in silence, ready to make the detritus of the day magically disappear. I am invisible.

"I'll be working from home tomorrow Sara, it's in my diary. I'll have the BlackBerry on if anyone needs me. Just want to get my head down and finish this…" Tom wheels out his usual Thursday apology whilst the others shuffle and pack their bags.

Sara rolls her eyes, not needing to hear the rest. Tomorrow she will be alone with her computer whilst these overpaid schoolboys most likely play golf. She gives Tom a brief nod, and Paul and Andy the most begrudging of smiles, before turning her back.

Dismissed, Tom heads out into the daily surge for the station. The anxiety will be rising in his chest as the minutes close in on the 5:32 to Skipton. As the train doors close I imagine him still at the ticket barrier, the guard showing no mercy for a misplaced season ticket even though he has seen it every day this month, including this morning. Tom will dig in his pockets for the exact change as he curses the ticket machine. At least this will keep his mind off the interrogation he faces. Sometimes these take place at home, other times they are by phone when the office is empty, save for the non-person emptying the bins. In his household, a missed train somehow equates to a sordid office affair or a stealthy beer to avoid family duties. That in turn translates into at least twenty four hours of blame, guilt and the cold shoulder. I picture him looking at the departures board and wistfully imagining that he has in his hand a ticket for the Highland Sleeper.

By this time, Paul will be safely on the train to Halifax. As his fellow commuters open the latest Dan Brown or close their eyes to another alternative reality, Paul will remain fixated on his BlackBerry. The board meeting will just be finishing, and with any luck, the Chief Exec has had the chance to table his report. His report, but his name appears nowhere on the discarded drafts in the paper recycling bin. Even after a solid ten years of service, he remains faceless and nameless. I can hear the ping from here:

"Great work, Paul. Only had time to mention briefly at end as people needed to get off. Need supporting info re. policy and more on financial implications. Please have with me for 9am tomorrow."

Paul will want to slump but there is no space. Nor is there any room for negotiation. It will be a long night, made even longer by the baby that never sleeps.

Cleaning his desk, I glance out of the window and see Andy sloping off quietly into the car park. Four days in the office and he is at his limit, tomorrow is either a day at home or another day sick. The medication helps, a pack stashed in his desk drawer in case of emergency, but the stigma must cancel out the benefits. It can't be easy being labelled the office nutter.

And Sara? She will sit alone on Friday, queen of all she surveys. Which is mostly eBay.

HOME TOMORROW?
by Jordan-Levi Rowlands

The Uncouth.
People speak of houses where they lived.
I called mine home. Because I have left does not
remove the title home, for me at least.

It was and always will be a house for everyone to see, but to me
and a select few it is our home.

But now I have no home.

Lose a few bets, gain a few enemies and end up on the dirty
grime floor of society's ills.

Living upon rubbish heaps.

Rotting with the best of them.

"Living like a common pest," the ignorant people say.

Look closely you naive idiot, it is me, your neighbour,
your friend.

You cross the street. You avoid my stare.

You ignore my pity. Yet I am the uncouth fiend.

Where does your conscience sit? When did it leave you behind?

You will get my just revenge.

Karma will scupper you, my friend.

My new home is coming, I can see the day and hear the
music sing.

I can feel the end of pain. I can see my home again.

The Opulent.
Some homeless person stared at me today.
Is the street really his home?
Home?
I've never had a home.
I had a place to sleep, eat and live.
It was never home

He looked at me incredulously, begging me for help.

I think he thought he knew me, but I showed him erroneous.

I meandered across the street. Still walking on.

"The end of the world is nigh. Home tomorrow is hell on earth," said another vagrant flea.

A mother passed, dropping some change and a business card for a local church drive, dragging kin behind her. Two young girls both on way to the large shop up the road.

She sets a bad example, teaching young girls to help felons and pill pushers, paedophiles.

'They' will never be urbane.

I then realise something – the lout from before is my ex-neighbour.

Ah yes, that guy. His beautiful wife took solace in my arms.

I acquired her in my bed.

She was not ready to be poor.

Now she, like he is out of my life.

And I am still Opulent.

The Compassionate.

"Fool," my husband bellows when I get home that night.

"They will spend it on drugs and booze, never food," said my youngest, repeating her father's previous rants.

I become outraged. I am not a fool. I am compassionate and I believe we should help the less fortunate.

"How dare you pollute our children's views with the likes and stereotypes?" I had been on my feet all day, my children too, handing out tokens and cards for our local Shelter.

I believed things should improve.

I abhor any man whose greed has enveloped his charitable nature. I want a better future,

For not one but all, including the unfortunate soul.

If it was up to me, here in my house is where he'd be and me in the streets.

But alas the home of tomorrow may never be.

ON THE CARDS
by Sarah Scott

"Hi! It's Lesley. I came back because Michael told me to find you. He's my angel. He is different from my husband Michael, because he's Mick. Can you help me?"

"I can try," said Tanis and she smiled at the woman she had never met before, putting her book and a half-eaten teacake under the counter.

"You're a witch, are you?" Lesley's voice was an overloud monotone.

"Well, I know about stuff, like crystals and tarot cards and oils. I haven't got a cauldron, though."

"I need a crystal for luck. I'm moving into my place. Claire bought me a duvet cover and my Dad is borrowing a van next week. It is lovely. I need a crystal for luck."

"Well, luck's a tricky thing. Some say that jade is lucky. Amethyst is good for attracting angels." Tanis was aware of someone outside the door, watching them. A carer, perhaps.

"I need protection as well because even when Mick's out, he's not allowed round. I need to have luck and know the answers. Do you believe in fairies? Maybe I should buy some fairy cards." Lesley eyed the sprawling deck on the counter.

"I think your angel sent you here because he wanted me to tell you to save up your money for your new house." Tanis said, gently, ever-mindful of karma, even though it never seemed to pay her back for the good. Her next reincarnation had better be bloody good. This place was dying, slowly, taking her life-savings with it.

"But I need to know when they're coming home. Michael won't tell me and Mick says I'll never see them again because I'm a nutter but I said now he's gone they will let me see them and I asked three packs of cards, with angels, unicorns and mermaids on them but the answers are always different."

"Maybe you're asking the wrong question? Or you don't like the answer they're giving you? Buying a new set can't make what you want to happen, happen."

"Claire said that. I just want to see my boys though. They took them off me ten years ago. They'll be thirteen and fourteen now. No, eleven and thirteen. They said I couldn't cope. But he's gone, isn't he? It's safe now and clean and everything. I just need to know when they can come and stay." Lesley looked mournfully towards the door, where her companion was tapping on her watchface.

"No pack of cards will tell you what you don't want to hear. One day, maybe they can come home tomorrow, but you have to be strong today. Here, have this. For your new flat." She pressed a slightly chipped amethyst bead into Lesley's sweaty hand.

"I have to go."

Tanis watched her leave. Now wonder this place is going to the dogs, she thought. I'm giving the stock away. But she made a silent wish for Lesley, waiting forever, for her stolen children.

DEMOLITION
by Margaret Scragg

A stout spider meanders along my dusty windowsill, stops, explores films of grease clinging to glass panes, like cataracts. The majority of my ceilings are netted with fractures and only too willing to sprinkle clouds of dust over the shoulders of suited surveyors in Bob the Builder hats. These men fist my walls, poke sticks at loose plaster, discuss my fate. And because I am old I have no say in the fact that maybe I will not be a home tomorrow. I will be rubble.

Their safety boots grind my rotting staircase and, once the banister feels the warmth of their soft palms, it spears them with splinters. A choir of expletives shoots from their mouths like hailstones, disappear through wide cracks in my one time magnificent, magnolia walls. A bulky-bodied bloke enters my bathroom, stands by the window, blocks the sun, prods a black-capped biro into decomposing putty around the stained sink. A fair bit of the plumbing is suspect but my U-bend is to die for and has never let me down once. Never blocked or leaked in all of my 84 years. A hard-hatted geezer checks the stained legacy of two incontinent bath taps while voices in the living room gather force, compare notes, laugh, joke about pinpricked skirting boards, say only mice could throw darts that high. I curse silently as they mock, and then a conditioned postman forces junk mail through the rust pimpled letterbox. The distraction arouses enough curiosity for a five foot surveyor to tamper with the flap of the box. The flap bites, sandwiches his manicured hand, his sausage fingers. My response, totally trimmed with delight, echoes every expletive he barks. He stands open-mouthed as his words bounce right back to taunt him. He opens the door, frees his fingers before randomly scratching paint from the weather-beaten wood. Once again his colleagues cry with laughter; they watch with interest as he digs deep lasting wounds into the dodgy hinged door. The laughter grows, filters through the rooms. His fellow workers move on to the living room. They mock nicotine stains, white patches of wall recently relieved of paintings, mirror and clock. A single, frosted lamp bulb watches from the ceiling. Beneath one geezer's hard hat, flared nostrils give way to uncontrollable sneezing – his nose is a dust sprinkler. The ceiling crack they prodded in the passage earlier widens by the minute. A piece of plaster the size of a paving slab thuds to the floor. The shrill of a telephone confuses me. I am disconnected. The boss with the blood pressured face holds on to his hat, starts acting crazy. His frog eyes bulge. His lips hover over his mobile phone before he shouts. Top priority, everybody out, death trap, demolish ASAP.

I shake uncontrollably when safety boots start the stampede.

HOME TOMORROW
by Mark Simpson

Texture is most important; you don't want baby's delicate skin scratched and scraped by some cheap horse-hair rag. Quality, that's what matters. It's my one little luxury – clothes shopping for my daughter. It's nearly spring, so pastel colours are a must. I follow my daily ritual of laying out clean, beautiful clothes. Her room smells lovely in the mornings, and the pale sunshine dapples and plays there as I stand still, watching.

It's Tuesday, and I'm already behind, yet endless fatigue makes even the simple things an effort. So much to do, and I've not even started on the backlog of mail. Can't face that today, there are things that must be done. I stop at the top of the stairs, frozen for a moment, gripping the rail till my knuckles turn white. A random mail drop startles me. "Damn letters! Why must they keep coming?"

Coffee doesn't soothe like the smell promised, and I brush past forgotten tasks in the kitchen. What time is it? Mummy and baby bonding time is overdue. I bundle all I need into the pristine pushchair, and make my way out, laden heavily, as all good mothers should be. It's a cold sun that fails to warm me, and the unforgiving buggy jars my hands on the rough, abandoned streets. I buy the daily provisions, unthinking, and haphazardly arrange them in the spare seat space.

It's a steep climb through the fresh-cut grass, and already my eyes are red and puffy. How rash the gardener is to cut so soon the short-lived stalks. Oh, how I long to walk through wide fields of tall, slender grass. Grass that had a chance to reach for the sun and be all it could be.

Before long, it is time to stop and arrange things for our time together. "Nappies!" I cry, and begin a frantic search through every pocket and compartment till I find one. I laugh at myself for the few moments of hysteria I have indulged in – it is not uncommon for new mums to be like this, I tell myself.

Kneeling in the mud and stubble grass, I lay the new garments out carefully, with fresh flowers too, singing gently the lilting melodies that all good mothers should know, till a song forms inside me and I sing once again to Stephanie:

"New clothes, my sweet baby girl,
In such a place of sorrow…
And bright yellow daffodils too,
For you'll be home tomorrow…"

HOME TOMORROW
by Cath Smith

Home tomorrow, after being liberated. Three years spent in a concentration camp, living on nothing but cabbage water and literally starved. All I remember of Dunkirk was a blast and me lying on the beach in agony. My arm had been blown off and all I could think of was "I'm going to die". I was slipping in and out of consciousness.

I woke up in a makeshift hospital, some nurse by my side. I learnt I'd been captured by the German enemies and was now in Stalag XX1. Taking a fearful glance at where my arm had been, and tightly bandaged, I broke into tears remembering the last time I was home on leave, holding my beautiful wife in my arms, her face happy and smiling. We talked of our future together, our hopes and dreams, something to keep us going through the dark days of the war that had separated us from each other, something to look forward to when all this was over!

Through those years at the camp, I learned to live with one arm and the stump that was my other. I wrote to my wife as often as was allowed, even though every word was scrutinised. I sent a postcard to my sister Susie, who wrote and told me she would keep it for sentimental reasons; maybes it was because of the Stalag XX1 postmark, who knows!

A lot of my friends died in that camp and I shall never forget them, their faces once filled with hope, filled with despair. I have Jimmy Docherty's possessions in my keeping, to give to his wife, just small mementoes. A lock of her hair that he carried around in a small tin, a photograph and his wedding ring secretly hidden away in a corner, still covered in bits of dirt. He told me where it was, the night before he died. Good friends, too many lives lost, years of fighting and bloodshed and for what? We fought for peace in a changing world, hope for the future. It should never be forgotten, lest all of those good men would have died for nothing.

The sun is coming up, it's been a long journey. I can see the white cliffs, we're approaching Dover. A new day is dawning. I can't wait to step out onto English soil again. Wonder what my wife will think when she sees her once stocky built man now a shadow of his former self, minus an arm. Still, I'm lucky to be alive and I'm on my way home with a good future to look forward to and a wife who loves me. What more could I ask for!

HERE COMES THE SUN
by Mick Snowden

"Calm down, Sarah," crackled the Co-ordinator's voice over the subspace radio.

"Calm down? CALM DOWN? Have you any idea how important this is?" yelled Chief Researcher Magrane.

"I do. And I'm sorry we have to cancel the shuttle. But we're expecting a Coronal Mass Ejection sometime over the next 72 hours, and it's probable that it will affect the entire Euro Zone. We just can't risk it. Co-ordinator Bartram out."

Magrane felt a pithy retort building, but knew that hurling it at the now silent subspace mouthpiece would feel hollow and empty. She chose instead to punch the console next to the mouthpiece, conscious of the need to refrain from damaging the vital link to Earth. The door behind her whispered open, and Magrane turned to face the newcomer, purposely swallowing down her rage. After all, it wasn't the fault of anyone on the Research Pod.

"Yes, Researcher Traviss. Please have some good news."

The junior researcher could tell that Magrane was in a foul mood, and frowned slightly.

"Well, the best I can do is that it's lobster thermidor on the lunch menu today. Other than that, it's just a whole bunch of 'no further progress', I'm afraid."

Magrane let out a heavy sigh. Sixteen months they'd been on the Lunar Research Pod – currently Euro Zone's only major space research project. They were trying to discover a way to either manage or dissipate the harmful plasma surges caused by increased solar activity. In that time, the entire power and data infrastructure of the eastern seaboard of North America had been lost, and the Japanese and Chinese had been severely disrupted.

Every lead, every new approach, had resulted in precisely zero progress. And in sixteen months, Magrane had asked for precisely one week's leave. And now the very force they were trying to control had directly scuppered her. She was starting to take this personally. How could she do otherwise? Peter Magrane had laid down the ultimatum. Either she was home for their daughter's graduation, or as far as he was concerned, she could stay on the Moon forever – and the divorce papers were already prepared, ready to be filed.

A thought occurred to her.

"Traviss? Has anyone made any attempt to repair the emergency transmit booth?" she asked.

"Are you serious? They're cancelling shuttles left, right and centre at the moment. Why on earth would anyone want to have their molecules scrambled when a plasma pulse could sweep them away in an instant?"

"You're not a family man, are you, Traviss?"

"No – married to my research."

"Then you wouldn't understand. But is the booth operational?"

"I think so."

Sarah reached a decision.

"I'm going. Now."

Traviss gaped at her.

"Do you want to die?"

Magrane's face creased into a sardonic smile.

"If I don't get home tomorrow, my life's over anyway."

Magrane gathered the bag she had prepared, and slung it over her shoulder.

"Wish me luck."

THE CITY OF HOPE
by Kate Stephenson

John stands beneath the clock in the Central Station. It was from this spot, thirty years ago, that he had flung a final goodbye before jumping on the King's Cross express, driven by rage and pride. There was no pride left in him now. Was he the prodigal son returning home? He breathed in; not today he wasn't. Leave that for tomorrow. Today he would rediscover the city. During all those long years in London he made sure never to come back, relentlessly denying his heritage. The ability of such a man to bear a life-long grudge is awe inspiring and tragic. Bitter worms had eaten away at his soul; each day he became more immune to humanity. Then without warning came a cataclysm, bankruptcy, collapsing his life into a black hole. Distilling all the lies, delusion and posturing into a small soft ball of phlegm. In one last monumental tirade it spewed forth, spraying all to the winds, until he had sat childlike, alone. Free from a self-made prison. It was need that drove him to the city of his birth.

Wrapping his coat round himself, John ventures out into the worn streets. A cold biting wind strips down all remnants of his protective shell. Panting up the hill, golden buildings loom over him. Pink cheeked, with drops of sweat lingering on his brow, he reaches the summit. Stopping, he strains to see the apex of the tall grey monument, an echo of reform and transformation. Senses open and raw, he spasms at the taste, smell of fear swirling round him. Scared whispers pass from person to person, heads down, clothes clutched fast as they scurry by the strange juddering clown. A howl of joy splurges from his mouth. To be here, now, was exhilarating. The whole city was vibrating with trepidation. Electricity hung in the air, ready for discharge. The storm of change all poised and ready to go. The only anchor left was faith. Faith in the endurance of the ancient city.

Exhausted, he slumped down, his back supported by the monument. Tomorrow he would visit his Mam. Hoping to be forgiven, praying that his new-found humility might repair the rift. Too long had it taken for him to understand the solidarity of family. How proud his Mam had been when he'd got into Cambridge. Soon it was a wedge. His family became uncouth, uneducated, naive fools who rejected progress. What had his sophistication and arrogance got him? A trophy wife, who took the money and ran. Sparkling friends who evaporated once insolvency beckoned. The result, breakdown, homelessness. Alone in the capital. But now he was back. Back to find a home, his true home, a family home. Was this too much to wish for?

THE FLAT
by David Stringer

He wiped orbs of cold sweat from his forehead with the back of his left hand, and with his right lifted a bottle to his dry lips. Sucking down only air, he looked through translucent green to check he'd emptied the contents. Climbing to his feet, he planted a peck on her cheek, and placed a hand softly on her shoulder, as she steadily and therapeutically brushed strokes of pink onto the far wall.

He shook the bottle, she responded in the negative to his question, placing a hand on her still thin stomach as she replied. Finding the sternness on her pretty face amusing, he teased her for following doctor's advice so early. Reacting swiftly, he jumped through the door just in time to avoid a paint-stained rag thrown in his direction.

Laughter made his voice dance as he moved through the flat, teasing her preparation, her seriousness, until he was out of earshot.

He reached into the mini-fridge on the kitchen table, alarmed for a moment that there was little light, and even less beer. He then realised how much the room was taking shape – her brother had brought in the dishwasher during the day, the ceiling lamp was shaded, the mini-fridge's taller cousin was whirring rather than sitting silently. Opening the door he found his ambrosia, sharing a shelf with raw red meat and microwavable meals, above bland vegetables and below gulp-sized bottles of probiotic yoghurt. He'd have to get used to compromise.

He took out a bottle, and an opener from the drawer – one of five pieces of cutlery they owned. She had promised to bring her own implements over during the day; it wasn't like her to be less than exhaustive. He took a sip and smiled to himself – he'd tell her she had baby-brain. He mentally braced himself for a whack to the arm as he thought of it, he could almost feel the pain in his mind's shoulder, but that just made him laugh more.

Childishly amused by the small wit his silly mind had created, he was unable to keep a goofy smile from giggling up onto his face. He detoured through the flat to the hall. (Foyer? living room? It was the first time he'd lived in a flat with more than one room…)

Something was wrong. Where was Ali? There was a space on the white wall, noticeable only for it's sameness, for lacking a print of Cassius Clay beckoning Liston to rise.

We can't have that in the front room… It's an iconic moment of sporting greatness!

He began searching for where the strong-minded minx was holding him captive. In looking around, at the uncarpeted floor, scattered plates and DVDs, the Ikea parts… he thought of the future that lay in this place, a future of domesticity and silly disagreements, arguments he wouldn't mind losing.

He took a long sip as he looked ahead.

It was a flat today, but a home tomorrow.

ONCLE EDOUARD
by Chris Talbot

Edouard woke up but didn't open his eyes. The world looked strange – alien – to him when he looked around, so he mostly kept them shut. He knew he was very young, his body shook with each breath. He was lying on his brothers and sisters, all was warm, comforting. The memories of home were stronger when his eyes were shut.

Sometimes – especially at night, in the sweetly enveloping darkness – Edouard remembered the view from his window. He remembered the way that the old tree tapped on the panes of glass when the wind blew. He remembered the faded green paint that was gradually losing its battle with the elements, revealing the weather-warped wood beneath. Yes, in the dark of night, when sleep was upon him, Edouard could almost remember…

With the dawn, the ghost-memories shimmered like morning mist then vanished, replaced by the ball of hunger sitting in his belly. They were feeding him watery milk and he craved meat. Edouard stretched a paw over the hot scrum of small bodies and opened his eyes. He had been blind in his first new memories. Blind and deaf, those early weeks had been a time of constant suckling and fierce introspection. That was when he had remembered – truly known – who he was.

"Chad! Descend!" Edouard heard the voice of the over-mother and leapt.

"Descend!!' Toujours 'Descend'!" Edouard answered grumpily, feline vocal cords turning the words into "Broo! Brooang? Broo!"

He landed, almost gracefully, on the kitchen floor and padded his way into the carpeted living/sleeping area. Occasionally he still remembered what it was like to be human, to be old, on his death bed, looking out of the window as the rays of a strong African sun slanted into the room at the top of his niece's house. He had been Oncle Edouard then, but he was Chad now. The name made his whiskers twitch into what would, on Edouard's face, have been a smile, for it had once been the name of his country.

At his most sentient, Edouard's fur had rippled with fear, his man-mind terrified by cat-form. He missed his intellect like a phantom limb, cat tongue imprisoned his soul. His human memories, fading for the past year, now resembled dream-like snapshots, frozen images. He had been black then, and was still black now, which would console him, except now his blackness was fur and not skin.

Edouard's language had been French and the over-mother (as he thought of the woman who had loved him ever since he had left his cat-mother) spoke French. He appreciated the effort she made to do this, even if his feline physiology made it impossible to reply. This saddened Edouard when he thought of it – which was seldom as his disappointment at being mute was more than made up for by the joy of having a tail to chase. Maybe, he thought, it was all a dream and he'd be home tomorrow or, perhaps, tomorrow he'd call this life home.

HOME TOMORROW
by Lucy Taylor

I am pure consciousness.

I observe curiously but have no words for what I see. A grid pattern of whiteness encloses me.

Sound existed before I saw although I paid it no attention; a steady pattering noise, non-threatening. There is constant movement within the white, made up of many small objects. I inhabit space and have limits that the small things hit: I am something.

I observe the exterior of my form. The surface contrasts with the white in a shape that brings no sense of recognition. I know of two things: me and not-me. I categorise, although without words. I have distinct form, different to the white under me, and my sight dispassionately considers my exterior. Soft, irregular. I compare and contrast. My eyes range on to where BANG there is a WHAT? a line across YELLOW and reddish-purple and BLACK STITCHES and I recognise out-of-placeness, and even as the shocking colour words form I suddenly have all my words; I can name everything because I recognise my scar. I have had an operation, I'm in the shower, in Hexham hospital.

I close my eyes and feel warm water falling on me. I recognise this, I am in the shower, lying half in and half out. I know what and where I am, even if the details are yet to emerge.

I call "help" tentatively. I barely hear myself. I shout "help" twice. I have never shouted for help before and it seems dramatic and attention-seeking. Nobody comes.

I'm on my back, half in and half out of the shower. The curtain is hanging to the side and there is water pooling on the floor. The floor isn't clean, and I've had enough. My limbs are working but my stomach muscles aren't. I get up, rolling over with the pregnant-lady ooooh noise. There is no particular pain, but I am awkward in this body.

I don't want to fall again. Behind me there is a seat, a washbag, a dressing gown and towel. My shampoo is on the floor and I touch my hair; it feels soapy. I must have tipped my head back to rinse, forgetting about my low blood pressure. Shouldn't that be normal now?

I am shivering now, so I turn off the water and put on the towel and dressing gown. The door is unlocked and I see a corridor and a nurse.

I tell her I have fainted and she walks me back to my bed. My husband is sitting with our baby wrapped in a blue blanket on his chest. I knew it was going to be a boy, I remember that. Everything will be there in my head when I'm ready.

People come and feel my head for bumps, take my blood pressure. I'm doing well; we can go home tomorrow.

Nobody wants to know what it felt like, not knowing what I was. It was okay actually.

THE RETURN
by Ian Todd

The band had been on tour for months. I always enjoyed the first few weeks but then the gigs got boring and I just wanted my own bed. It was always a dream of mine to go on tour and play my music every night to crowds who adore you. That isn't always the case as we found out in Manchester when we ran away from a bunch of angry Chav types.

Chloe is always waiting for me when I get home; we go and get a takeaway and watch boxsets of the latest American drama series she is now obsessed with. People change and I hated being away as I miss the everyday, the evolution of the self. I have to catch up with all my friends, having an iPhone and Skype doesn't stop you lusting after normality. Memories of the tours started to get a bit blurred as we have another Burger King and toilet stop.

Everyday seems to merge into one; every city is a replica of the last date on the tour. Maybe I was just too old for this life. At the age of 31, I want an easy life. It used to be exciting in the old days, groupies and getting drunk, not that I ever did either. I sit and wonder what Chloe is up to.

It's the little things I miss, the sound of her laugh, her cheeky smile. Not long to go until this bloody tour ends. I might quit the band after this tour. I just don't enjoy it anymore. I spent my days thinking of home. I have been in the band for five years now and we have had some fun but all things come to an end and anyway I'm just the bass player.

The tour ended. I am relieved. It was a great tour and we have loads of new fans but my life has to be about more than this. Maybe start a family, move to the country, read more books and get in touch with my Dad and patch things up. I got home to an empty flat. There was a picture of Chloe on top of the freeview box. That's all I have left of Chloe. It was one year last week when she passed. It's good to be home.

HOME: A TRAVELLER'S COLLAGE
by Cila Warncke

London, England, 2007

L ondon, England, 2007
"All knowledge is borrowing and every fact a debt. For each event is revealed to us only at the surrender of every alternate course," writes Cormac McCarthy. Am I ready to surrender the alternate courses? At what point do I let go of the possibilities and embrace the continuity of rent, bills, an eighteen-month phone contract and waking up next to the same person every day? Love is marvellous, slippery, fragile, hard, and possible. It is a collection of years, hours in pubs, grocery shopping, trips to Venice, tears, arguments, flirtation, cups of tea, bus rides, watching the darts. Inconsequential moments multiplied to create something greater than the sum of their parts. Love: the only home neither time nor distance, disagreement nor disappointment can ever touch.

Ibiza, Spain, 2008

"I would be happy being a peasant," I tell my flatmate as we sit on the terrace. "I would be quite content eating lentils, quaffing red wine and going to bed when the sun goes down." There are days when I even believe this. I long for routine. A home shaped by the physicality of baking bread, peeling vegetables, and sweeping sand from tile floors. A place surrounded by the things I love, where I can be still with someone who might understand me.

Mérida, Mexico, 2009

To work, I need a place to call home. Here, on the crumbling outskirts of Mexico's erstwhile richest city, I've found one. It is sticky-hot. Yesterday I killed a cockroach as it ran laps in the sink. A cat yowls outside and the internet connection goes up and down like one of those fairground rides they strap idiots into before flinging them skywards on giant rubber bands. But my room is large, with a hammock slung across the middle and a long wooden table ready to be littered with books, pens, notepads, sunglasses, water bottles, and dictionaries. My new home smells of drains and the swimming pool is dry. But around the corner is a tortilleria where I can buy a dozen rich, earthy-smelling corn tortillas for two pesos.

Glasgow, Scotland, 2010

The predicted high is minus-one. Moving anywhere, doing anything, is a struggle of will in this weather, an effort to escape the tedium of dark-grey cold. There is no beauty in the heavy sky. The wind is not a soothing murmur. It cuts you up, slaps you around, snatches at your feet. A friend and I take refuge in my flat. We fill the high-ceilinged kitchen with the sound of Neil Young and the smell of nine solid hours of baking Christmas cookies. Chocolate chip, gingerbread, sugar cookies, almond crisps, apple turnovers, marmalade-filled thumbprints and chocolate espresso fudge. We drank wine and eat macaroni cheese. My friend is a version of my younger self: an earnest American with a sweetly apologetic demeanour. She is a good girl, as I once was, striving to make a home. Will it be easier for her?

HOME TOMORROW
by Joyce Warwick

There was no getting away from it, his face was going greener. From his floating bed under the cyberpool on the ceiling, Zog glimpsed his vivid green face. Fancy going home tomorrow, green all over, under his spacesuit. Mojo, the craft's cyborg, was bright green too – he didn't care as he lived on board the spaceship.

Mojo had helped him find and carry those horrible green plants back to the ship and probably contaminated them both with green! Anyway Mojo had now minimised the plants, the train, the aeroplane, the hovercraft and car and stored them away in a miniscule locker ready for regeneration back home on reaching their lovely planet Rainbow.

Sometimes on their forays from Rainbow they had ended up quite furry, or skinless, short of a limb or two and once he'd even lost his third eye. But a session in the lab with Mojo's ministrations usually got him back to normal, but now this green wouldn't go away!

His beautiful mauve wife Zita and all the pastèl coloured Zoglets would probably disown him. She hated green! Probably to do with that ghastly green Chlora, the home-wrecker. Even though he'd never looked her way! No one liked Chlora.

The pool in the ceiling took on a silvery hue and tall, slim beings just like Zog smiled down on him. Heavenly music played as he slipped into his deep coma which preceded his return to Rainbow. In the pace of one whole Earth day, the ship was transported the three zillion miles to planet Rainbow. It coasted down gently through shimmering rainbow dust and landed with a soft plop on a gas cloud.

How wonderful to be home! Descending from his spaceship, he discarded his breathing equipment and took in great lungfuls of the sweet, pure gases. His wife Zita and all the little Zoglets came to greet him with outstretched arms, as if he'd been missed! As he reached to hug them he was amazed to see the horrible green had disappeared! Purple! He was purple again and they loved him still.

JOHN: HOME TOMORROW
by Victoria Watson

She's coming home tomorrow. She says she's coming home to level everything out, start over. After all these weeks, all the phone calls and the tears, all the begging and the pleading, she thinks she can forgive me.

It was all such a stupid mistake; I can't believe I even did it. Shirley's my wife, why almost ruin it for a quick fuck on a photocopier? Sure, she hasn't been the same since the kid was born but she says that's no excuse.

I'll have to ask Rick for tomorrow off. I'd better be there to meet her. I need to show that I appreciate her coming back. I need her to know Hilary meant nothing.

I know what's coming next, she'll ask me to move on, leave the bank. Oh, sure, it's okay to say that but what would I do? She'd soon change her mind once she realised the cars would have to go, the summer house would have to go, her whole life would change. My whole life would change. No platinum cards, no interior decorators, no future. Maybe I can get Hilary moved. I'll speak to Rick, he'll help me out. He's been there, haven't we all? As long as we don't fire her, there'll be no tribunal. It's a big place. We'll be able to get her moved and get me a new secretary, sure.

It's a sunny day, not a cloud in the sky. I've got a spring in my step; I've really dodged a bullet. Losing my wife could have been bad for the job too, they like you to have a pretty thing on your arm at corporate things. Preferably the same pretty thing. And we all know what pretty things like: money. Why else would Shirley be with me? Let's not kid ourselves. I'm forty fucking five, I'm bald. I look like that guy from The Sopranos. She's twenty-nine, legs up to her fucking neck, blonde hair down her back. C'mon, man, I didn't get to where I am by being that dumb.

I'll need to call the cleaners, the florists, maybe Tiffany's. Yeah,

Tiffany's, she'll like that. Get a big new toy for the kid, not that he'll notice. Kid don't speak, kid don't show any recognition. Money can't buy you everything, huh?

The TVs are on in the reception.

"Good morning New York, today is Tuesday, September 11th 2001 and you're watching Fox News. It's 8am on a beautiful day, here's your news…"

I go into the lift and press the button, Floor 81. Yeah, I'll speak to Rick, Shirley will be home tomorrow and everything will go back to how it used to be.

HOME TOMORROW
by David Wright

Dad broke me camera. A Kodak Instamatic 110 with a cube flash on a stick. He was meant to be a photographer, he did this for a living, but he wound it on too far and jammed it.

I sat in my bedroom, the crook of my arm over my eyes to keep the light out and the tears in.

Downstairs the party just carried on – Stephen, Mum, Dad, Uncle Tom, Auntie Vera, Pauline, Angela and Julie laughing, chatting, drinking Blue Nun or green pop.

I had the bedroom at the top of the stairs, just enough room for my bed and a wardrobe. I had a record player in there but that was it. There was no room for anything else.

Shirley Bassey was on the stereo, always Shirley Bassey. Every time people came round it was non-stop Big Spender and Goldfinger.

Dad loved these house parties, telling the same stories to the same people.

He still tells them now, but now the laughter has gone, the joy drained away. A life of memories lost in a mind that doesn't work anymore.

Mum reminds him everyday who he is, about me, my brother and the kids.

Then the stories will start – getting bombed out, being in the police, swimming with Joe Magoo. One after the other, stopping to eat, and then over again. Mum listens.

All I can think of is the broken camera. I hated him then. Laughing at me, telling me it was rubbish anyway, that I'd get something to cry for. Then starting again with the tale of the sing-song breaking up the fight in The Jawbone, standing on the bar, police helmet under one arm, using the baton as a microphone, singing 'Underneath The Arches' 'til the fighting stopped, proud that everyone went home and no-one was arrested. I knew it like I'd been there myself.

Now he cannot remember his wife's name but the party stories spill out like a reflex.

I'll be there tomorrow, going home, letting my Mum have a few hours off. It will be the same as always, Shirley Bassey playlist and sitting with my Dad. I'll still go upstairs when the tears start, sit in my room and then back downstairs. The Joe Magoo story, trying to laugh like it is the first time I've heard it.

Tomorrow I must tell him I love him.

TO SAY GOODBYE
by Scott Young

As the clouds fell from the sky into the tundra that was the grey horizon, Katy smiled for the first time in fifteen months. It had been a long time since she'd felt as safe as she did in this moment, her whole journey now held in one sun-faded plastic carrier bag.

Children played below laughing as the water licked their heels and tickled their toes. Their games and songs reminded her of the avenue by the open park back home, where the children would no doubt still chase each other in the spring.

Looking out across the bay, thoughts wandered from things unsaid and sailed off towards the small rowboat as it came into sight. The breeze felt somehow warmer on her face. It was time to leave everything behind.

Her father's grave would be long overdue some care.

Katy looked forward to spending some time there, a place where she could finally sit and talk freely. A knowing that with each word another wound would heal and finally disappear.

A familiar tune caught in the breeze from below, a song from a time when all things were different. Katy heard herself singing along, not remembering what the next words were, as if on autopilot allowing herself to act involuntarily for once.

A pair of purple shoes stood next to her pulling on her sleeve to interrupt her from her hymn.

"How do you know that song?"

"Sorry?"

The child could have been no older than six years of age. Her face held all the innocence of childhood just as it should, with eyes open and wide ready to feast on the world.

"That's the song my Daddy used to sing to me."

Her words rang true like a spear through Katie's heart.

Looking up, she saw the rowboat now still and waiting for her at the water's edge. A final moment passed as she stepped down from the balustrade onto the pebbled promontory. She handed her last scrap of tired notes to the skipper in exchange for a hand aboard the gentle craft slowly bobbing beneath her feet.

As Katie settled into the bow with her old bag and a prayer, she readied for her journey home. A tear fell from her cheek as she watched the shoreline disappear, knowing that as the distance fell further away a new beginning came closer.

She was leaving for the first time, a journey she had thought so often of so many times before. Finally strong enough to return home, finally healed enough to say goodbye.

Katy reached into the carrier and removed the precious cargo from their plastic mausoleum. Holding them she knew that she had carried them as far as she should, it was now time to let them rest.

The sun sang merrily that following morning, the trees appeared greener than any tree had looked for years as a woman placed a pair of small purple shoes by her father's grave.

Writers' Block North East

Writers' Block North East is an organisation based in Middlesbrough which was set up in 2010 to train and support creative individuals and businesses, and to find ways for them to work together.

Writers' Block hosts regular training events to teach writers new skills. It offers networking and business-to-business opportunities, introducing creative people and their work to industry professionals. It provides the facilities and resources to enable writers to get their work in to print, on film and performed to an audience, and opportunities for writers to work alongside emerging creative professionals including actors, crew, animators, musicians and artists.

Writers' Block is run by Laura Degnan and James Harris. Laura is a writer/director working in film and theatre. James is a comedy writer, performer, animator and filmmaker. Writers' Block is supported by Middlesbrough Council and the European Regional Development Fund.

For more information visit **www.writersblockne.com** or email **laura@writersblockne.com**

Out Now from Sixth Element Publishing

Residual Belligerence by C.G. Hatton
Paperback, 256 pages, RRP £6.99, eBook £1.49
ISBN 978-1-908299-03-1

Tension and intrigue combine with classic sci-fi adventure in the first book of a series set within the knife-edge universe of the Thieves' Guild.

Blatant Disregard (Thieves' Guild: Book Two) is due out in Nov 2011.

Screw, God and the Universe by Graeme Wilkinson
Paperback, 284 pages, RRP £6.99, eBook £1.49
ISBN 978-1-908299-06-2

Screw, God and the Universe is a darkly funny tale of death, sex, violence, booze and religion that could well be the wayward child of Brett Easton Ellis and Terry Pratchett and is sure to get the pulse racing (or at least vaguely bamboozled).

Disturbing Bedtime Tales (For Very Bad People)
by Dean Wilkinson
eBook, RRP £1.49 • ISBN 978-1-908299-16-1

Disturbing Bedtime Tales is an anthology that takes the medium of the fairytale and fable to new dimensions of dark and twisted, comedic surrealism by award-winning comedy writer Dean Wilkinson.

Home on the Range by Susan Lewis
Paperback, 136 pages, RRP £12.99, eBook £6.99
ISBN 978-1-908299-00-0

Home on the Range is an enthralling and poignant account of life in Billingham during the 50s and 60s. Susan Lewis tells of growing up during a time when the tranquillity of the small village is transformed into the hustle and bustle of an industrial town by the chemical giant ICI.

Sixth Element books are available in paperback from all good bookstores, and in eBook format from Amazon, iBookstore and Smashwords.

Visit www.6epublishing.net to buy direct from the publisher.